Loving

FIC
HOS

Loving

Published in 2020 by Seoul Selection U.S.A., Inc.
4199 Campus Drive, Suite 550, Irvine, CA 92612
Phone: 949-509-6584 / Seoul office: 82-2-734-9567
Fax: 949-509-6599/ Seoul office: 82-2-734-9562
E-mail: hankinseoul@gmail.com
Website: www.seoulselection.com

ISBN: 978-1-62412-139-5 52700
Library of Congress Control Number: 2020946652

Printed in the Republic of Korea.

* *Loving* is translated and published with the support of the Literature
Translation Institute of Korea (LTI Korea)

Loving

Translated by Brother **Anthony of Taizé**

Jeong Ho-seung

Author's Preface

Coming down from a visit to the recumbent Buddhas
on the hill above Unjusa Temple,
I went and stood before the temple's main hall.
Suddenly I realized that there was no sign
of the brass fish that should have been swinging
beneath one of the wind chimes at the end of the eaves;
only an empty wire was left dangling in the breeze.
I felt curious as to why, for what reason,
that fish had gone away.
Finally, I wrote this tale
and realized why there is a breeze blowing in my life,
and why no wind chime can be heard,
where my being's proper place was.
And so I was able to forgive myself.
The breeze is blowing.

I dedicate this tale to the wind chime of Unjusa Temple.
I also dedicate it to lovers who
by loving one another
become one another's wind chime.

Jeong Ho-seung

Returning from a visit
to the recumbent Buddhas at Unjusa Temple,
you brought back with you
a wind-chime, hanging
from the eaves of your heart.
If a breeze comes from afar
and you hear the wind-bell chiming,
understand that my heart,
longing to see you,
has come visiting.
—Hanging Up a Wind Chime

Freedom. . .

Love's wind chimes. . .

A pine needle, borne on the wind, strikes sharply against my side, then drops toward the ground. It's a fresh, green pine needle, blown all the way from the distant pine grove that surrounds the two recumbent Buddhas. Before the pine needle can reach the ground, I emit a clear, ringing chime which goes rising up into the blue sky. When my body sways in the breeze which brought the pine needle, the small, cross-shaped clapper, which was waiting for me to move, rocks in turn and strikes against the inner side of the bell. And that is transformed into a clear sound, ringing serenely in every corner of the hillside shrine.

My chime settles on the blades of grass growing in cracks of the rocks behind the main hall, even reaches as far as the bowl of rice offered to Lord Buddha inside the temple hall. On spring days, there is a sound of fresh shoots sprouting in the bamboo thicket. In autumn, hoarfrost crackles as it settles on the fallen leaves. In winter, the crunch of lonely human footsteps echoes along the snow-covered trails.

There are quite a few monks who cannot sleep if they do not hear me. If people who come to visit the temple cannot hear my voice, they fail to find peace and their hearts leave the temple before them.

No one dislikes me or the sound I make when I shake in the wind, a cool sound, so clear as to seem transparent. There are even some city folk who hang one like me up on their apartment balconies and wait for the wind to blow.

Those who have guessed will already have understood that I am the fish hanging beneath a wind-chime bell attached to the westerly eaves of the main hall of Unjusa Temple, which lies in Hwasun, Jeollanam-do Province, the far southwestern region of Korea. I am made of a thin sheet of copper, but clear blood courses though my veins. My tail is constantly twitching, and a breeze from afar sets my fins trembling as though I'm flying. I have a pretty name, too: Blue Bubble-Eyes. Another wind-chime fish hangs from a bell at the eastward end of the eaves: Black Bubble-Eyes.

Black Bubble-Eyes and I met thanks to a monk from Seoul's Jogyesa Temple. In those days I was hanging all alone from the ceiling of a shop in Insa-dong which had a signboard saying: "Buddhist Supermarket." I recall it was the afternoon of a day when the first leaves, barely the size of a human fingernail, had begun to emerge from the gingko trees along the street side. A monk came into the shop, gave me a gentle nudge to test my sound, then told the owner he wanted to buy me.

"It'll be just right for Unjusa's main hall," the monk declared. "A lovely sound. The head monk will be delighted." As he spoke, the monk smiled in satisfaction.

I had no idea what the monk's smile might mean but in a flash I was taken down from the ceiling and prettily wrapped in pink mulberry paper. But just before I was enclosed in the paper, something quite unexpected happened. The female shopkeeper opened the door of the storeroom where various Buddhist goods were kept and produced a wind-chime fish just like me and laid it on the counter.

It quite took my breath away! I had never dreamed there might be a double, just like me, shut away in the dusty storeroom wrapped up in newspaper.

All that time, feeling extremely lonely, I had been longing for someone. I had been praying for a genuine meeting with someone I might spend the rest of my life with. Would I ever meet them, that someone who would fill up my days? I had been wondering whether I would ever meet someone who might fill my entire lifetime, whether there existed someone whose whole life was being diligently lived in the hope of meeting me?

The shape of our lives can vary greatly, depending on whom we meet. Life is a mosaic of meetings and partings. But so far I had not experienced even life's most basic kind of meeting. Inevitably, I was utterly amazed to find that a wind-chime fish just like myself had been shut up in the storeroom, only waiting to meet me.

I calmed my racing heart, looked at him, and waved my tail.

"Hello!"

"Hello!"

He looked at me and waved his tail, shaking the dust from his scales. If my eyes were blue like an autumn sky, his were black as the last night of the waning moon.

"You need to have names. Since you're a carp with protruding blue eyes, you can be Blue Bubble-Eyes, and you have protruding black eyes, so you'll be Black Bubble-Eyes."

After the monk had given us our names, he put us into his gray knapsack.

We were stowed together in the monk's knapsack as soon as we'd met. Thrilled to have met my true partner, who I hoped would fill my whole life, I never noticed how suffocating it was inside the knapsack. I could only give thanks that the meeting I had so earnestly prayed for had at last come about.

On the day the monk hung us from the opposite eaves of the main hall in Unjusa Temple, he told us:

"Now don't go quarreling. You must get on well together."

Since that day we have lived as the wind chimes of Unjusa's main hall, facing each other and chiming in the breeze.

I still cannot forget that thrilling moment when I first met Black Bubble-Eyes. I cannot forget the warmth of that moment when he first embraced me inside the monk's knapsack.

Meetings are mysterious. Love, too, is mysterious. It's with a meeting that each of us begins to write the tale of our lives.

When a pine-wind blows, my voice has the fragrance of pine needles. When a clay-wind blows, it has the smell of the yellow-clay fields of Jeolla-do Province it brings speeding over. On spring days when a flower-wind blows, there is a scent of azalea petals; when a maple-wind blows in autumn, it has a trace of crimson leaves.

The people from Hwasun who come to visit Unjusa Temple all know that. They only have to hear the sound of my bell to know what kind of wind is blowing across Jeolla-do Province.

I like the flower-wind best of all. When the flower-wind blows I feel that I am really alive.

Today a flower-wind is blowing. A single azalea petal has been stuck to me for quite some time. My body is giving off a faint scent of azalea petals. But my heart is forlorn. Forlorn, too, are the robes of the stone Buddha who stands across the way, silent with hands joined before his breast, like a woman hiding behind a pine tree watching a man set out on a long journey. Where now are the thousand Buddhas and pagodas which a wonder-working monk is said to have erected in a single night, a thousand years ago?

I am lonely although I'm with Black Bubble-Eyes. Lonely, my body rocks in the wind. And today of all days I can see neither the farmhand Buddha guarding the recumbent Buddhas, nor the Lotus Blossom Pagoda.

Black Bubble-Eyes's heart has changed. At some point he grew indifferent to me. If the wind blows he only sways perfunctorily; if the sky is dazzlingly bright, he remains placid, merely blinking slowly like a calf.

Even if I chime just for him with a sound as delicate as that of a *geomungo* zither, he ignores it. Even if I dance just for him, with the sad motion of falling leaves when only he can see, he does not bother to watch. Even if I harbor a smile like a water lily in full bloom just for him, he remains expressionless.

It didn't use to be like this. Now, we don't keep the promises we once swore to keep. He promised to absorb the warmth of the midday sun shining on the yard before the temple hall, then send it over to warm me when the temperature dropped at nightfall, but he no longer does that. He promised to absorb all night long the starlight scattered by the lovely stars of October, then pass it to me when I was feeling gloomy the next day, but he no longer does that. We promised that when we saw a shooting star, we would each make a wish on the other's behalf, before it disappeared beyond the horizon, but he no longer does that.

He almost never calls my name anymore. Even if he does call out to me, "Blue Bubble-Eyes," I can detect no trace of affection in his voice. When morning brought the first snow of winter falling, covering Unjusa Temple in a layer of white, he used to shout, "Blue Bubble-Eyes, wake up, quick! Look, the first snowfall, the first snow!" but I no longer hear such exclamations.

Yet when he looks at Red Bubble-Eyes, who is hanging from the eaves of Vairochana Hall, the expression in his eyes is different. An expression brimming with warm affection, the way he used to look at me. When the wind drops and all is still, his eyes are invariably fixed like arrows on Red Bubble-Eyes. Maybe he's in love with her?

The present moment is so important in love. It takes wisdom to treasure the heart's present moments when in love. Ah, Black Bubble-Eyes has changed so much. Is there no such thing as a love that never forgets how the heart first felt, that never changes?

Surely we became one on the day we first met, sharing one another's body and heart inside the monk's knapsack, neither of us claiming precedence? Surely, on the day we were first hung from the eaves of Unjusa Temple, that day when a monk picked up a hammer and hung the wind chimes from the eaves, how happy we were. Our chimes were clear and transparent like the autumn sky. That night, listening to our chimes in the moonlight, hadn't Unjusa's stone Buddhas all danced, rocking their shoulders? Had Black Bubble-Eyes already forgotten the monk's bright smile that caressed us, and his words, "You are now one body. Be kind to one another"?

The day is overcast, as it so often is. A chill wind continues to blow, delaying the arrival of spring. I long to warm my chilled body in Black Bubble-Eyes's embrace. But he only rocks indifferently in the dust-filled early spring breeze.

Here and there snow remains unmelted. I can see people who have come over the remaining snow to visit Unjusa Temple, writing their names and prayers on new roofing tiles. One young woman writes on a tile in white ink, "May my wish be granted." What could she be wishing? Maybe she too hopes to meet the one person who will be able to fill her whole life?

Birds go flying across the sky. I long to turn into a flying fish. I've heard that in a mural from Goguryeo times, fish are shown flying about in the sky. I too long to turn into a fish that can fly freely through the blue sky. Just hanging like this from the eaves of a roof is no life at all.

Time went by, a period as long as that which I had already spent with Black Bubble-Eyes. I was still suspended from the eaves of Unjusa's main hall. Spring came, with cold spells at its start, winter came, and violent blizzards raged, and I spent my days one after another without the slightest change.

My life is so boring. Enduring boredom is immensely painful. I spend more and more days doing nothing, not even dreaming. I fully realize that this today, which I spend doing nothing, is the tomorrow which the person who died yesterday so longed to see. Yet still, I spend more and more days doing nothing. Do I really have no better life to live than one hanging from a roof?

More years passed. The agony of loneliness and boredom grew deeper. I made even greater efforts to love Black Bubble-Eyes. When night fell and clouds veiled the new moon, I would stretch out a hand all the way across and fondle his front fin, his most erogenous zone. As the stars faded one by one at dawn I would gently pour into his breast the purest starlight I had accumulated in my heart during the night.

Of course, love demands effort. Clearly everything is only achieved with effort. Unfortunately, though, effort alone is not enough when it comes to loving.

"I don't understand why our love has grown so lukewarm. There's no electricity flowing. Nowadays you don't react even if I hold your hand."

Whenever I said something of that kind, Black Bubble-Eyes would reply, "That's the way it is with old love," then stay silent for a long time.

"Why don't you say something?"

It was only when I fretted, shaking my tail, unable to endure his silence, that he would open his mouth again.

"When love is new, at first there are plenty of words.

But old love happens in silence."

That was how he always was. And I was always dissatisfied.

"We're not in love, and we're not not in love either."

One night, I woke him from a fitful sleep. Struck with the thought that if life is ultimately a mosaic of meetings and partings, things being as they were between us, it might be better to part.

"Black Bubble-Eyes, let's break up. I reckon that would be best. It's not right to deceive one another about our feelings. It's a waste for us to go on living like this. I don't want to live the rest of my life like this."

Once I had said all that in a trembling voice, I started to feel that breaking up was the natural thing to do.

"Black Bubble-Eyes, love is warm as sunshine, hot as sunlight. But your love is like dried up bird droppings. Love that's dried up and fed up isn't love at all. Have you ever seen the way birds flock to perch on a dead tree? Living together when you don't love each other is a crime. Only those who love each other have the right to live together."

I kept repeating my arguments in favor of breaking up. He made no reply. No matter how much I insisted, he merely smiled.

"We never had any proper wedding before witnesses, did we? We can separate whenever we like."

Unable to endure his silence, I started to shout:

"There's nothing to stop us, we can break up whenever we like!"

Black Bubble-Eyes finally opened his mouth slightly, as though sipping water from a pond.

"Blue Bubble-Eyes, have you forgotten the moment when the monk hung us up here? That moment was our wedding ceremony. The sky and the wind and the grass, the birds and the clouds and the flowers all congratulated us on our wedding. They were all living witnesses to our marriage. You're completely misunderstanding something."

"I'm not misunderstanding. What sort of a marriage is this?"

"We fish always have this kind of marriage. It's not really what you would call a marriage. Living together as we do is a marriage in itself. Stop talking about breaking up. Some things in life are cut-and-dried in advance."

"No. You're wrong. Life is something you make for yourself. There's nothing fixed or determined in advance. Especially not love."

"You're wrong. Our love is part of our pre-determined life. If not, we would never have been able to meet as we did, love each other for as long as we have. Meeting you has been the greatest event and the greatest happiness in my life. Just being together with you like this always makes me happy and grateful."

Unlike at other times, Black Bubble-Eyes's eyes were shining brightly, like black pearls.

"Are you telling the truth?"

"It's true."

"No, you're lying," I spat angrily. "If you loved me, how could you be so indifferent? I've spent countless lonely nights alone."

The moon had risen bright in the sky.

"It's not indifference; it's just a matter of maintaining an everyday routine. As love goes on, it stops being as exciting as it was at first. It grows placid and peaceful. Even the finest fragrance becomes disgusting if it does not vanish but lasts on and on. It's only if it fades in a flash that it's a genuine fragrance. Love's just the same. When love lasts for a long time it turns into a kind of friendship, like friends spending a whole lifetime together."

What Black Bubble-Eyes said was not wrong, so I

made no further reply. Just as love is not achieved with words, as he claimed, so parting was equally not done with words.

"Blue Bubble-Eyes, do you realize what parting is? Parting is like dying."

I spent a year pondering his words. During that year, he did not greatly change. He never tried to embrace me and would fall asleep before me, before the stars themselves.

Every night I gazed up at the stars alone until I fell asleep. Or rather, I gazed up at the stars alone and rang my wind bell all night long. I was lonely. Black Bubble-Eyes could not understand my loneliness.

"I understand you," I told him. "Loving means understanding. The depth of love varies according to how much understanding there is."

But although I explained it to him, he could not understand me. Just as I could not understand him.

When the cold winds of early spring began to blow, I once again began to insist that we should part.

"We can each have our own separate life. We can have better lives than we have now."

"What life do we need apart from the one we have now, Blue Bubble-Eyes? For us, the most important thing in life is to give happiness to our neighbors by chiming beautifully in response to the will of the wind."

His tone was both subdued and affectionate. But my love for him had already grown cold.

"No, Black Bubble-Eyes, that's not all there is. I want to go flying across the sky. I want to set off for somewhere. Hanging here like this is really burdensome for me now. I've started to dream of flying through the blue sky to my heart's content. I truly do not want to abandon that dream. The size of one's dream is the size of one's life. So why don't you have any dreams? Why are you satisfied with a life spent just hanging here like this?"

"Why do you say I have no dream? My dream is to

live an ordinary life, loving you and bringing joy to those around. To you such a dream may seem small and insignificant, but to my way of thinking it's the greatest dream in the world. My hope is for you to dream the same dream as me."

"Out of the question. That's just your dream. I don't want to be your dream's partner. If you truly loved me you would help me achieve *my* dream."

Black Bubble-Eyes looked at me in silence for a while. Maybe he was listening to the rain, which had begun after the new moon had set. Something like sadness was gleaming in his eyes.

"If, I, truly, love you?" Black Bubble-Eyes stammered.

"Yes, if truly you love me!" I said in a rush.

The wind blew. The rain grew heavier.

Black Bubble-Eyes abandoned himself completely to the rain and wind, shaking wildly as if in agony. It was the first time I'd ever seen him shaking wildly, letting himself go in a storm.

It seems that the wind and rain will never end. I long to pierce them and go flying somewhere far away. Is there really no way out of my present life?

I twisted my head round and stared for a long while at the mountain ridge to the south, wondering whether the recumbent Buddhas had stood up and were taking a stroll. They were a pair of stone Buddhas lying unfinished on an enormous, 13-meter-long slab of rock. I knew that they were a married couple who enjoyed taking a walk, holding hands, unseen by anyone. Just before sunrise, as dawn began to gleam on distant Mudeungsan Mountain, the two of them

would rise and walk along the trail through the pine grove together. Simply watching them from a distance was enough to make my heart swell.

Today, perhaps because of the rain, instead of going for a stroll, the recumbent Buddhas are simply lying there in the rain. But the husband Buddha is lying slightly turned to one side, with one hand raised.

"Why are you holding your hand up like that, Recumbent Buddha?"

I spoke with a rain-soaked voice.

"I'm sheltering my wife so she doesn't shiver in the icy rain. I've done the same for a thousand years, whenever it rains or snows."

I suddenly felt faint. I had never dreamed that the husband Buddha might love his wife so much.

"So is that what love is?"

"Yes, this is love. Blue Bubble-Eyes, do you know why I am still an unfinished Buddha, even after a thousand years?"

I remained silent, uncertain what to reply. Without waiting, he continued:

"It's because love is always unfinished. There is no perfected love in this world. There is only the process of perfecting love . . . love is the continuation of that process."

The recumbent Buddha kept his hand raised, keeping off the pouring rain. The cold rain struck the back of his hand but he paid no attention.

"And what is parting, Recumbent Buddha?"

Once I had decided to part from Black Bubble-Eyes, I had been invaded with fear. I wanted to ask the recumbent Buddha how I could rid myself of that fear.

"Parting means not being able to see someone when you want to see them."

"Is not being able to see someone so frightening?"

"Parting is something frightening, when the heart yearns for what it cannot see. But whenever there is meeting, there must also be parting. Don't fear parting too much. Parting, then meeting again—such is life."

The rain continued to fall. The drops were so thick that they seemed melancholy. Even if I parted from Black Bubble-Eyes, I did not think he would long to see me. If partings were to be feared only when the heart longs to see the other person, then it seemed that I would be free of fear so long as I did not long to see him.

"Recumbent Buddha, there are times when I want to be a breeze shaking a wind chime."

"Then you are forgetting your duty. If flowers wanted to become roots, what use would they be?"

"Still, a life spent hanging from the eaves is terribly painful."

"Your heart is the problem."

"Sometimes I want to turn into a flying fish and go flying through the sky. How can I escape from this dangling life and gain true freedom?"

"That too is a matter of your heart. The problem is that you do not truly want it."

"Recumbent Buddha, I do not truly want it, you say? That's not so."

I joined my hands before my breast devoutly, like the stone Buddhas, and looked up at the recumbent Buddha.

"No. It's not what you really want."

Continuing to shield his wife's face from the falling rain and not lowering his hand, the husband Buddha looked down at me as though he felt sorry for me.

"I will ask you something. Two monks are watching a flag fluttering in the wind, and they are arguing. One monk says it's the flag which is moving, not the wind, and the other monk claims it's not the flag moving but the wind. Which of them do you think is correct?"

"Well . . ."

I had no idea how to answer. But when I considered the problem from my own perspective, as a wind chime, the answer seemed relatively obvious.

"It's the flag that's moving. Just as I move when the wind blows, the same principle."

"Is that really so?"

"Yes, it is."

"No. It is neither the wind that moves, nor the flag. The only thing that is moving is the fractious hearts of those arguing monks."

I automatically bowed my head at the reclining Buddha's words. Everything seemed to grow bright before my eyes, as when dark night is over and dawn breaks.

The problem lay with my heart. If I truly wanted to become a flying fish, if I really wanted to attain true freedom, the recumbent Buddha assured me, I would be able to attain them. But I had no idea how I could make myself truly want something.

The rain stopped and a fresh breeze came blowing. I remained hanging from the eaves, quivering in the fresh green breeze. Spring was back, but as ever Black Bubble-Eyes gazed at me with an indifferent gaze.

Still, in my heart a lamp was burning bright. Although I did not yet know the method, the thought that I could attain what I wanted so long as I truly wanted it ensured that my heart ever tended the wick so that the lamp in my heart would not go out.

One day a swallow came visiting and tapped me with its beak.

"I want to build a nest here, beneath the eaves of the main hall; will it be okay, do you think?"

As the swallow looked at me, I saw my own image, swaying in the wind, reflected in her eyes.

"Okay. Come and build."

I shook my body with joy and gave off a sound of petals blooming.

"Will it really be okay? Won't the monks be against it? Suppose they're angry that someone has built a house in this pure and sacred place, then what?"

"They won't be like that. If anything, they'll be happy."

"Well, I'm not so sure about that . . ."

The swallow turned in circles beneath the eaves, clearly worried and unable to come to a decision.

"Well, let me ask the recumbent Buddha."

I turned my head towards the southern ridge and fixed my eyes on the recumbent Buddha.

He raised his upper body very slightly and nodded twice.

"He says it's okay. He says that no one has ever built a house here before, but you're not to worry and build it anyway."

"Thanks."

The swallow gave me another tap with its beak before flying off.

While I waited for the swallow to come back, a new lamp was lit in my heart. Waiting eagerly for someone is like lighting a lamp in your heart.

It was only several days later that the swallow returned with her mate and diligently set to work building a nest. Dozens of times a day they would arrive with mud, straw, or twigs from somewhere in their beaks and started building.

Just as the swallow had said, they built their nest directly below the eaves of the main hall. They began to build a house shaped like a tiny crock on the fascia boards, which were painted with a multi-colored lotus pattern.

As soon as the swallows began to build, the faces of the monks coming into the hall for the dawn chanting grew bright. A silent smile hovered on their lips, as though they were recalling the homes they had left behind. Even Black Bubble-Eyes' placid gaze seemed to have recovered some of the gloss of the time when we first met.

On the day the nest was finished, I gave out a special grass-blades sound I had been saving up just for the swallows.

Once the eggs were laid, the swallows took turns flying across the blue sky. I envied the way they could fly freely through the air.

After the eggs had hatched, the swallows flew about even more busily. I didn't know where they were getting them from, but until the veil of night fell they kept arriving with beaks full of insects, which they pushed into the gaping beaks of their young. When the mother swallow brought food, the babies would open their beaks wide and chirp loudly with hunger. To me, that sounded even more beautiful than the chimes of Black Bubble-Eyes and myself.

Then, one day, as a mild spring breeze was wafting across from Mudeungsan Mountain, and Unjusa's stone Buddhas were dozing languidly, I was trying to keep the sound of my chiming as quiet as possible so as not to wake the Buddhas and watching the nearby swallows' nest.

One baby swallow had poked its head out and was

peering down into the hall's front yard. There was no sign of the mother; she must be off gathering food somewhere. The baby swallow's newly sprouting down was utterly charming. I watched the baby for a while. Suddenly I felt a longing to become the caring mother of a cute baby like that.

Then it happened. Perhaps it was hungry, or maybe it was looking out for its mother, who was still not back. The baby swallow lost its balance as it poked its head ever further out of the nest and started to fall.

In a flash I hurled myself toward it. My only thought was to save the baby. Luckily, I was able to grab hold of it just before it struck the stone steps of the hall.

It burst into tears.

"Don't cry. It's all right, it's all right. Your mom will soon be back."

I carried the baby swallow gently up and put it back in its nest.

But something very strange had happened. I had not realized as I went flying after the baby swallow, but suddenly my body and mind were feeling newly light and free.

I quickly glanced up at the end of the eaves I had been attached to. The bell still hung there, but without

43

the fish, which had fallen off. There was no fish, only the wire the fish had been hanging from was swinging to and fro in the wind.

Why, I was flying through the sky! I had finally become a flying fish and freed myself from my old life of dangling from a roof. When I had gone flying down toward the yard, intent only on saving the baby swallow's life, the wire fixed to my dorsal fin had snapped.

I understood that the moment for me to part from Black Bubble-Eyes had arrived. From the moment I began to fly he had been gazing after me in confusion, his eyes bulging even more than usual.

"Hello!" I cried, circling beneath the eaves.

"How did that happen?"

"I'm a flying fish now. Look. I can fly."

Black Bubble-Eyes watched as I went flying this way and that. As I moved my fins, they gradually turned into wings, propelling me forward. He was so shocked that he couldn't stop gaping.

"I'm leaving here."

"Leaving?"

"Don't try to hold me back. It's what I've been longing for."

"But where will you go?"

"I've only stayed hanging here because I didn't know how to obtain what I truly wanted. But now I'm free. I've gained my freedom. I realized that I could obtain what I longed for when I helped others."

I flew rapidly to the stone lantern standing in the yard before the main hall.

"Blue Bubble-Eyes, don't go! This is where you should live!"

Black Bubble-Eyes screamed at me. I did not look back, as though to say I would never come back.

"Blue Bubble-Eyes, I beg you not to go . . ."

I could hear Black Bubble-Eyes sobbing.

I left the yard and headed for the southern ridge, where I bade farewell to the recumbent Buddhas. There was no knowing when I might see them again

"I'm leaving. I'm going out into the wider world to become a real fish."

"Farewell. You have gained your freedom. But be careful. With freedom comes responsibility. If ever you want to talk, wherever you are, no matter how far away, I'll be able to hear what you say."

The husband Buddha pulled out the arm that his wife's head had been pillowed on and waved.

"Come back whenever you want to. I'll be waiting.

Our bodies may be far apart, but our hearts at least will always be with you."

I could still hear Black Bubble-Eyes's tearful voice.

Pretending I could not hear him, I left Unjusa Temple. I left Black Bubble-Eyes's side.

This life in which I could fly excited me so much that I didn't care where I went. Unjusa Temple soon vanished from sight. Hwasun disappeared. I went on flying, high and far.

"Blue Bubble-Eyes!" someone called. "Where are you going?"

I turned to look back, and it was the wind that used to shake the wind chime.

"I've no idea."

At that I realized I had been overcome by the sheer fact of flying. I slowly calmed down. My eyes took in the surrounding view. I was flying somewhere high up and looking down at the great Jirisan mountain range; the Seomjingang River looked like a thin curved line drawn with a pencil.

Ah, I'd flown too high without realizing. Suddenly I felt afraid. Where should I go?

"Wind, where's the best place for me to go?"

"Where do you want to go?"

Perhaps because I was looking worried, the wind took me by the hand.

"I don't know. I've only been longing to be able to fly; I haven't made any kind of plans so far."

"Then think about it now. Where do you want to go? It's your first time, so I'll go with you, just this once."

"I hadn't realized going on a journey would be so frightening."

"Ha ha, don't be too frightened. It frightens everybody. No one can live without fear."

The wind laughed heartily and pushed against my back. Suddenly I thought of the sea, the smell of it, that fishy, greenish tang I'd occasionally detected on the wind as it shook the wind chimes.

"I've got it!" I shouted, excited again. "The sea! I want to see the sea. Wind, please show me the way to the sea."

"Right. Good. The mere sight of the sea should serve to show you the meaning of a life with wings."

The wind pushed against me again. I threw off my fears and set off flying toward the sea. The sea was a long way away. Sometimes I lost the way, then found it again.

How far had I flown? Gradually the strength was ebbing from my wings. Actively flying through the sky was many times more demanding than passively hanging from a roof. Perhaps, after all, holding on and waiting for what you want is less difficult than hanging on to it once you've got it.

I flexed my muscles and mustered my courage. There was no one to help me now. The wind had only shown me the way to the sea, then at some point had left and was nowhere to be seen.

How far had I flown now? I began to smell a fishy, watery tang, the same as the wind had sometimes carried all the way to Unjusa Temple, then in a flash the sea lay spread out before me. The moment I saw the sea, I exclaimed "Ah!" It looked as though someone had laid an enormous piece of blue silk cloth over the ground.

I flew closer to the water. The gentle rippling pattern of the waves was breaking white in the sunlight. I felt acutely that I had escaped from my stationary life and was now flying freely.

I flew even nearer. The closer I came, the louder the waves became. When the waves threw themselves against the cliff, where a single pine stood facing the horizon, their sound was extremely beautiful. I landed gently on the edge of the cliff and stood beside the pine, gazing out toward the horizon.

The sun was setting. Red lotus blooms rose above the horizon. At first they appeared one by one, as if someone were pulling them quietly upwards and making them bloom one after another in the sky, then after a time a red blaze flamed up and consumed the individual flowers.

"I wonder what lies beyond the horizon," I murmured. "There must be something to make the sun vanish beyond it."

I kept gazing in fascination at the blazing horizon. At that, a plover sitting on the pine tree said, "There's an island beyond the horizon."

"An island? What's an island?"

"An island is like a stone separating one sea from another. It makes the sea more beautiful. The sea is beautiful because there are islands."

The bird was about the same size as me, our breasts were a similar silvery color, so we treated each other like the closest of friends from the very start.

"Is it far from here?"

"Very far. It's somewhere even I can't get to easily, though I live here on the coast. I went there once. My mother told me not to go. She said you die if you fly out to sea, so I went without her knowing. And I nearly died. However far I flew, there was no end to the sea. I flew on and on, there was only the horizon. The strength had faded from my wings, I was about to drop into the sea and die, when I saw the island. There was an island in the sea! If there had not been an island, I would have died. My friends likewise believe that you die if you fly out to sea. I taught them about the island, but they all lack the courage to go there. They don't even want to go. So I'm waiting for a chance to go back to the island alone."

The plover seemed to be on the point of spreading his wings and setting off.

"Then let's go together."

I longed to see the island that made the sea beautiful.

"Fine, let's go together!"

As a sign of approval, he shifted from a northward branch to a southward facing one.

The next morning, having waited for the sun to rise, the plover and I flew out to sea, in the direction the pine tree's branch pointed. The sea shone dazzling bright. For a moment I found myself thinking how wonderful it would be if Black Bubble-Eyes were flying out to sea with me, but the thought soon vanished again.

The plover flew at a fast pace. I went speeding after. But before we had left the seashore cliff far behind, a falcon suddenly appeared. It came diving down like a bomber plane, climbed again, then came flying straight at me. I abruptly regretted leaving Unjusa Temple. I nearly fainted at the thought that I was going to die here.

I mustered my remaining strength and headed for the cliff. The falcon followed without slackening its speed in the slightest. It was going so fast, surely, because it was convinced it could not fail to catch its prey. I turned away from the cliff. The horizon tilted. Just then:

"Get away! Quickly!"

The plover shouted urgently as it went flying toward the falcon. I headed back in the direction of the cliff and as I did so I saw the falcon's talons grasp one of the plover's wings.

It was all over in an instant. The falcon that had been pursuing me seized the plover in mid-air and wheeled away towards the cliff. There it began to stab the plover's breast with its sharp talons and beak. I was terrified. I feared that the falcon would come after me again. I left the dying plover with blood streaming from its torn body and sped away from the sea.

How far did I fly?

Jirisan appeared again, and far below, the curve

of the Seomjingang River, like a single white cotton thread.

At the sight of the river I grew calmer. I alighted on Seomhojeong Pavilion in Hadong, which has the best view of the river, and looked down at the water. Only then did I weep. I recalled how the plover's little wings had fluttered as he was seized by the falcon.

Why had the plover thrown away its life for me? What could I do for the plover in return? Had the plover somehow been the island in the sea that I had wanted to visit?

All through the night, I stayed perched on the roof of Seomhojeong Pavilion and gazed at the Seomjingang River. From the direction of Gurye a night bird could be heard calling .

Inevitably, morning dawned again. The Seomjingang River was showing a pure white surface that glittered unchanged in the sunlight. I perched numbly on the roof of Seomhojeong Pavilion, simply gazing at the wavelets. My first sight of the sea had been a shock, but then witnessing the plover's death had been a greater shock by far.

What is death? Why is death part of life?

All night long, I could not sleep. I could not speak one word to the stars. My first experience after leaving Unjusa Temple had had been death, not love.

I had never once thought of death while I was living

beneath the temple's eaves. Countless times I had seen the flowers beside the stone Buddhas and pagodas blossom and fall, but I had never once thought of that as death.

I had no idea where I should go, so I spent several more nights on the roof of the pavilion. When I felt hungry late in the afternoon, I would go down to drink a few sips of water from the river, then fly back up.

Time went by. Every night, the stars in the night sky shone, numerous as the grains of sand in the Seomjin-gang River. The more the stars shone, the more time flowed by.

It was time for me to leave the pavilion. But I felt that so long as I could not understand death, I would be unable to understand life and in consequence found myself unable to take a single step in any direction.

One night, I quietly asked the stars to summon the recumbent Buddha.

He came to me in the form of starlight.

"What is death, Recumbent Buddha?"

Without one word of greeting, I asked him what I most yearned to know.

After a long silence, the starlight Buddha replied:

"When you were a wind chime at Unjusa Temple,

there were days when no wind blew, weren't there?"

"Yes, there were."

"When the wind did not blow for a time, did you think that the wind had died?"

"No, I never thought that."

"If the wind drops for a while, does that mean it will never blow again?"

"No. The wind was sure to come blowing again."

"You see, death is like that. To say the wind has stopped blowing for a time is not to say it has died. You recently saw the sea for the first time?"

"Yes, I saw the sea."

"Did you see the waves?"

"Yes, I saw the waves, too."

"And did the waves break?"

"Yes, they struck against the cliffs and broke in white spray."

"The waves broke, but was the sea annihilated?"

"No. The sea was still there."

"You see, death is rather like that, too, like the waves of the sea. The waves disappear but the sea remains as it was. To say that there is death is not to say that there is no life. Just as waves are part of the sea, so death is part of life. So don't be too sad. Set off in search of true freedom."

The Buddha's starlight seemed to shine more brightly.

Gazing up at it, I felt I could understand death just a little. To say that the wind has stopped blowing is not to say it is dead—that was what I had always experienced as a wind chime. Many times, the wind would stop, then come blowing again and make my bell ring.

"But why does there have to be death in life?"

I could not stop but asked again.

The starlight Buddha was silent for a time before answering:

"Ultimately, it's for the sake of life. If there is no death, our life cannot exist either. It's because there is death that we all exist. Death is the result of life, life is the cause of death."

"But I can't understand why the plover died for me. Why did he save me and die himself?"

"You must think about that for yourself. The time has come for you to understand life and death."

The starlight Buddha vanished. The stars began to shine silently once more.

As I reflected on what the starlight Buddha had said, I fell into a deep sleep. Even as I slept, I could hear the sound of the distant river churning as it headed for the sea.

The sun was rising above the iron bridge across the Seomjingang River. As the sun rose, a train passed over the bridge. I followed the train for a moment, then let it continue on its way alone, alighted in front of the inscribed stone placed in front of Seomhojeong Pavilion, and quietly recited the poem "Hadong Docks."

80 *li* from Hadong Docks
waterfowl cry
as the moon rises
80 *li* from Hadong Docks
a man writes poetry

on the stone step of Seomhojeong Pavilion,

a dandy

who has left home to come here

I read aloud, focusing on the syllables one after another. Since the word "dandy" meant "a stylish, elegant young man," I imagined a young poet writing poems on the steps of Seomhojeong Pavilion.

At that moment, a young man came up and addressed me.

"You have a very good voice for poetry. Clear as a wind chime."

"Who are you?"

I took a swift hop backwards, then stopped, rather afraid at talking with a human being.

"Don't be frightened. I'm the person who wrote the poem on the stone that you were reading."

He was not very tall, with round, gold-framed spectacles, and a blue jacket.

"I've never seen a fish like you before."

After examining me closely, he suddenly offered to shake my hand. I did not brush his hand away. Anyone who writes poetry on the steps of Seomhojeong Pavilion must surely have a beautiful heart, and not be someone to be wary of.

"Why, you've got wings! How strange. I knew there were things called flying fish, but never expected to meet one personally. I'm very pleased to meet you, anyway."

He clasped my wing and shook it warmly.

"I used to play here at Seomhojeong Pavilion when I was a child. My friends and I played with marbles or pasteboard cards, right on this very spot! But tell me, what's your name?"

"Blue Bubble-Eyes."

"My, what a beautiful name. But you look wretched. Are you having problems? Are you sad about something? Do tell me. I'll write a poem to help you get over your sorrow."

Just as I'd guessed, he really did have a beautiful heart. Before I'd even opened my heart to him, he'd already seen right through me.

"A friend died in my place. A hawk was attacking me, and he made it change direction."

The moment I mentioned the plover's death, my breast was shaken with sobs.

"I too once caused the loss of a friend. When I was a child, I went swimming just over there beneath the bridge, slipped into deep water, and nearly died, only that friend rescued me. But once he'd rescued me, he couldn't stay afloat, so he died."

He gave my hand another squeeze. Both our hearts were aching at the thought of our dead friends.

"Why do you think the plover died for me?"

"Because he loved you."

The poet replied without a moment's hesitation, but I shook my head as if to say I could not believe what he said.

"We'd only met the previous day. How could he have come to love me in such a short time?"

"Love doesn't need very long, Blue Bubble-Eyes. Love sometimes happens in a moment, at first sight, in a flash."

"Yet still love needs time."

"Certainly. I'm not denying that. But more important is how you love, how much you love. Time is no use now so far as the plover's love is concerned."

I longed to see the plover. His love passed by like ripples on the Seomjingang River, piercing my heart.

"Even now, decades later, there are times when I find myself wondering just why that friend saved me then died himself. But no matter how much I think about it, it's always because of love. It was because he truly loved me that he died saving me. That's why I think that sacrifice is the essence of love. There can be no love without sacrifice. Many people are incapable of sacrifice and therefore are incapable of love."

We were silent for a while, looking into each other's eyes. In the poet's eyes the blue sky was hovering.

"Why, you have blue bubble-eyes too!"

He smiled brightly, perhaps finding my words amusing.

"Blue Bubble-Eyes, you need to learn how to give love. Some people only know how to receive love, but not how to give it. In that case, even the love they have received ends up being lost."

The poet's smiling face brought peace to my heart. That smile seemed to be inviting me to ask him anything I wanted to know.

"Sir, I don't understand why there has to be death even in love."

I still had many things I wanted to ask him. Living in this world brings countless questions.

"That's because very often it's only through death that love achieves its perfection. Several years ago, some first-year students at Jeonju High School rescued

66

primary school students who were drowning, but died themselves. That allowed me to sense the most perfect form of human love. Without love, how would such deaths be possible?"

"But surely, death isn't a beginning but an end?"

"Not so. Your relationship with the plover didn't end because it died. That bird lives on inside your breast still now, fixed in a loving relationship as ever."

"I don't know. I don't know how to live. I thought that a life flying around like this was more important than one spent hanging from a roof; now, on reflection, it seems that form is not that important."

"That may be true. The form life takes isn't so important."

"Then what is the most important thing?"

"Having a loving heart. The most important thing is giving your all for one you love. Loving is everything."

A breeze passed through the bamboo grove on the slope below the pavilion. I felt I could understand at least some part of what the poet had been saying.

The wind rises among the bamboos. The wind in the bamboo grove makes my heart tremble. I must live intensely the present day for the plover who sacrificed his all for love.

"Goodbye! Poet!"

I left the side of the man writing poems on the steps of Seomhojeong Pavilion and went flying toward the railway bridge.

I didn't have to wait long before a train passed over the bridge. I quickly landed on its roof. After passing through Suncheon, then Daejeon Station, the train finally arrived at Seoul Station, where it stopped. At least I now understood that the train had not died simply because it had stopped moving.

Seoul Station was full of the fragrance of lilacs. Crowds of people had come to greet those arriving. The fact that there was someone waiting when you arrived at a station I found very moving. The people welcoming took charge of the heavy bags, embraced those arriving lightly, then they set off together.

There was no one waiting for me. I had no idea where I should go. But my heart was swelling in anticipation of new encounters.

I slowly followed the smell of lilacs toward the post office in front of the station, from where the scent was coming.

When some homeless vagrants who were drinking on the station overpass spotted me, they shouted:

"Let's grab that fellow and enjoy some raw fish!"

I got a feeling that Seoul was a frightening place. I sensed that dangers were lurking 'round every corner. The atmosphere was completely different from when I lived in the Buddhist store in Insa-dong. Yet I vaguely felt that I did not need to be afraid. After all, I had already experienced the falcon's attack and the plover's death.

I spent my first night in Seoul like a vagrant, huddled beside some bins underneath Yeomcheongyo Bridge. I shed no tears. The lights of the trains heading off to the sidings in Susaek to sleep kept me warm. When the new moon rose between the tall buildings, I saw that even in Seoul the nights could be beautiful.

I spent several nights under Yeomcheongyo Bridge, fascinated by the passing trains. How beautiful the night sky would be, I thought, if trains could only sprout wings and go flying across it. The days sped by as I imagined what fun it would be if the train stations were in the sky, so that passengers would have to go up there to board and alight.

Then one day, a gray pigeon came flying down under Yeomcheongyo Bridge and addressed me.

"You've come up from the countryside, haven't you?" it inquired. "Not many days ago, I think?"

The pigeon kept turning its head from side to side, always on the lookout for food.

"How did you know?"

"I've seen you hanging around here for the past few days. You can't get by in Seoul just watching trains. You have to work hard in Seoul, if you want to survive."

"Seoul's so beautiful," I said, "and it feels even more

beautiful since you're here."

I changed the subject and tried to flatter the pigeon.

"I've heard people say that. But there are plenty of poor devils living in Seoul who can't appreciate its beauty. And the problem is, they're all the time growing in number."

The pigeon went on chattering, perhaps pleased by my flattery.

"I live on the roof of Seoul City Hall. Sometimes I go to Deoksugung Palace or come here, to the plaza in front of Seoul Station, looking for something to eat. But why have you come to Seoul?"

Whenever the pigeon's eye glimpsed something to eat it would peck at it, even in mid-phrase.

"I've come to Seoul to look for a partner. I hope to find my true partner in Seoul, one who would come out to meet me at the station if I arrived by train from somewhere."

"You mean you've come all the way to Seoul to find a partner?"

The pigeon looked as though it found that a rather weird thing to do.

"That's right, I've come flying all the way from Unjusa Temple, far away in Hwasun-gun county, to find my

true partner."

"Well, I'm not so sure you're going to meet another flying carp in Seoul. I've lived here a long time and I've never seen a carp that looked like you."

"So long as I really want to, we'll meet. I'm sure of it."

"I reckon you're too naïve. I live in Seoul and there are many occasions when it frightens me. Anyway, people will be glad to make a meal of you. One false step and you're done for."

Looking extremely concerned, the pigeon showed me its right foot. To my surprise, there was only one toe left on it.

"Do you know why it's like this? Because I got my toes tangled in a nylon washing line someone had thrown away. The blood couldn't reach my toes, so they rotted and fell off. If you're going to survive in Seoul, you need to be on the watch for plastic and string, above all. One of my friends ate some plastic. It got stuck in his throat and he choked to death."

While we were talking, several trains with their carriage lights off slowly passed on their way towards Susaek Station to sleep. Tonight, I thought, those trains are going to sprout wings and go flying about in the sky above Seoul. I also reckoned that somewhere in Seoul there was a carp waiting for me.

I spent a few more nights with the homeless people at Yeomcheongyo Bridge, then I left Seoul Station. Reckoning that it would be hard to meet my true partner there, I flew to Insa-dong at dawn. Insa-dong is the place where I was born and started to live for the first time, so it is no exaggeration if I call it home.

It being a Saturday, Insa-dong was thronged with young people. I walked among them, peeping into every alley. "I Feel Like Throwing Flowers," "My Husband Is a Woodcutter," "Singe the Moon with a Mosquito Coil"—the names of the bars and tearooms were so funny that I kept laughing.

Along one side of the street there were people selling antiques that they had on display. There were a host of things I saw for the first time in my life. There were bronze heads of Buddha, wooden clogs, charcoal-fired irons, and fulling sticks for beating laundry. I especially liked a small wooden lamp. I longed to light the lamp and read poetry all night long in a small thatched house near Cheonghakdong Village on Jirisan Mountain.

Since I wanted to keep seeing the lamp, I went to Insa-dong every day. Then one day a young mother came along with a little girl of kindergarten age and bought the lamp. I quickly followed them. They took the subway at Anguk Station, got off at Daechi Station, and went into block 19 of Eunma Apartments.

From that day on, I began to live near the parking lot in front of block 19. The parking lot was so enclosed that every time the cars blew out exhaust fumes, I had difficulty breathing, but the joy I felt on seeing the lamp lit was immense. The young mother used to get up past midnight, when most people's lights were out, and light the lamp. Then she would quietly take out a poetry book and read.

The sight of that woman reading poetry helped calm my mind. It was after I saw her that I came to think that human beings were more beautiful than I had thought.

> Now, no matter whom you love,
> love someone who knows when autumn leaves fall.
> Now, no matter whom you love,
> love someone who knows why autumn leaves fall to
>   lowly places.
> Now, no matter whom you love,
> love someone who can fall like one autumn leaf.
> On days when October's red moon has set
> and you long for a warm glow outside your window,
> no matter whom you love,
> love someone who can fall and rot like one autumn
>   leaf,
> love someone who can rot as one autumn leaf
> and wait for spring to come again.

Sometimes I would read in her heart the poem she was reading: "Now, no matter whom you love." Soon I could recite almost the whole poem by heart.

Of course I also grew close to her daughter. She had been attending the Eunma Kindergarten for less than a month and her name was Jeong Dasom. The world of

Dasom was always full of flower-like beauty.

When it was time for Dasom to come home from kindergarten I would go to the entrance of the apartment complex early and wait for her. Of course, she was also waiting for me. We became the closest of friends. I sometimes used to spend the time after she came back from kindergarten until she went to her piano lessons perched on her head, playing with her.

Along the road to Dasom's piano institute, here and there yellow dandelions were blooming. Dasom liked dandelions more than anything else.

That day, too, Dasom had come back from kindergarten and set off for her piano lessons after playing with me for a while.

"Oh, look, there's a dandelion blooming here!"

As Dasom was taking the crosswalk, she discovered a dandelion blooming right in the middle of the road and stopped.

The dandelion was growing in a crack in the asphalt and had just begun to bloom. It was truly amazing. It was certainly surprising that a dandelion should be blooming in the middle of the road, but it was also surprising that it not been trodden on by anyone until then and was blooming brightly.

Dasom glanced at the dandelion briefly as she crossed the road. But the green light was about to turn red. Suddenly, struck by some thought, she turned and ran back toward the dandelion.

"Dasom, don't, it's dangerous!"

I shouted desperately at Dasom. Perhaps she did not hear me, for she went running to the spot where the dandelion was growing and pulled it up by the roots. Just then, the traffic lights changed, a truck accelerated hard and sped forward without noticing her.

She fell. People came rushing. I sat on the branch of a sycamore tree and watched her fall, not missing a single detail.

Dasom was rushed to the hospital in an ambulance, still holding the dandelion clutched in her tiny hand. Two days passed and she did not regain consciousness. Sometimes, still unconscious, she would murmur, "Mom, the dandelion!" and grope around for the dandelion. Finally, after ten days, she died in the hospital.

Dasom's mother cried sadly as she planted dandelions on Dasom's grave. There was nobody who did not shed tears while they watched her planting those dandelions. It was the first time I shed tears for a human being.

Dasom had given up her life to save a dandelion. She had not been able to just stand by and see it run over and killed by a speeding car.

I felt that I could understand her. Just as the plover had sacrificed its life for me, she too had sacrificed her life for a single dandelion.

Still, I felt sad. I blamed God. I blamed God's actions: why should death be the consequence of true love?

Until one day, Dasom spoke to me. Dasom, who had just started to come alive in my heart, told me with a clear smile:

"Don't be too sad. Love is stronger than death, they say. You have to sacrifice everything for love."

For a long while I spent the nights in the vicinity of the parking lot of block 19 of Eunma Apartments, which no longer contained Dasom. Dasom's mom did not light the lamp late at night. I could no longer hear her moistening a finger and turning the pages of the poetry book as the hours went by.

The nights when the lamp was not lit were gloomy ones. However, I did not want to leave there until Dasom's mother once again lit the lamp.

While I waited every night for the lamp to be lit, I thought more about the nature of love that Dasom had revealed to me. I once again reflected deeply on the way love is accompanied by sacrifice in ordinary, daily life, and how love that is not founded on sacrifice is merely a sham.

Perhaps because of those thoughts, after experiencing Dasom's death, the face of Black Bubble-Eyes kept coming into my mind. Now he was all alone. I worried whether his wind bell was ringing properly and, if not, whether he might not be scolded by the monks.

I was amazed at myself. The moment I realized that I was still thinking of Black Bubble-Eyes, a corner of my heart grew bright like the sun rising.

A year had passed since Dasom's death. Dandelions were once again blooming everywhere. In front of the parking lot of block 19 of Eunma Apartments, too, dandelions bloomed yellow and smiled.

On seeing the dandelions I felt glad, as though I were meeting Dasom again. The moment the dandelions began to bloom, Dasom's mother lit the lamp. Late into the night, the sound of her turning over the pages of the poetry book could be heard. It had been only a short while, but time had the power to comfort her sorrow and make her forget.

I left the apartment complex when the dandelion seeds were blowing in the wind. I set off in quest of my true love. There was no need for me to be afraid about where I should go. Just as there is life where there is death, so too there is a road that begins at the place where one road ends. At present what I wanted was not to be loved but rather to love someone.

At Daechi Station, near Eunma Apartments, I took the subway to Suseo. Although I went down into the subway thinking how oppressive it was to ride a train that goes speeding along deep underground, unexpectedly I felt nothing of the sort. Rather, I enjoyed watching people hastily following the different arrow signs. I also hurried to keep up with the other passengers. Following them, at Suseo I transferred to the Bundang Line and got off at the last station. I thought it must lie well beyond the city limits.

I found myself in a forest, true, but not of trees. Instead I found myself surrounded by a forest of apartment blocks. I felt a bit disappointed but went flying down the road between the buildings.

The wind was blowing. Here too it was carrying dandelion seeds along. I flew on, following the dandelion seeds. And I landed gently at the place where the dandelion seeds fell.

There I found a crowd of people gathered around a

handcart, busily engaged in eating something. Among them were children like Dasom and adult women. I raised my head and looked up. I saw a roughly written sign, "Sticky-rice carp-cakes," and on the wire grill of a brazier in front of that, some carp were lying side by side, saying nothing.

At first I thought that they could not be real carp. But they were definitely carp. Their chests studded with dense scales, their protruding round eyes, their strongly bifurcated tails, their fins and the rest, all showed clearly the characteristic features of carp.

"What are you guys doing here?"

Glad to see them, I flew down and settled beside them. I suddenly realized that the brazier was very hot.

"What on earth are you guys doing, sitting in this hot spot?"

I addressed the carp closest to me, wriggling in the heat as I did so.

They simply lay there without turning a hair, as if the heat from the brazier did not bother them, and calmly replied:

"We're not carp; we're carp-cakes."

"What do you mean, carp-cakes?"

"Carp-cakes, that people eat."

"No, you're carp. I can't tell you how long I've been looking for you guys. I used to live in Unjusa Temple in the Hwasun area of Jeolla-do Province, then I came up to Seoul. You're the first carp I've met since I arrived here. I'm really glad to see you."

I felt my heart beating for joy. If the fire had not been so hot, I would have liked to have seized their hands and danced.

"No, you've got it wrong. Carp and carp-cakes are two different things. We're not carp."

They kept insisting that they were not carp. But I had a different idea.

"I'm glad to see you, anyway. Even though you call yourselves carp-cakes, still you're carp without the slightest doubt. Why else would you have been given that name?"

"Well, that's certainly true. When you put it like that, certainly."

Then some of them nodded and smiled at me. But the smiles soon turned to expressions of regret.

"You mustn't stay here. Run away quickly."

"Why?"

"With those wings of yours, you're clearly a very special kind of carp. Get away, quickly. You have to be afraid of people."

With one accord they shouted at me to get away quickly.

Just then, while I still did understand what they were saying, I saw something truly amazing. One of the carp that had been telling me to run away quickly was grabbed by someone's hand, bitten into, devoured. First, the part with the tail was bitten off and eaten, soon to be followed by the part from the chest to the head, until at last its entire body had vanished into someone's mouth.

It was all over in an instant. Yet still the other carp made no attempt to run away but only urged me to flee.

"You see? We told you. Get away quickly. What are you doing?"

"You guys run away, too. Why are you just sitting there like that without running away?"

"We are destined to die as soon as we are born. We were born to go into people's mouths, to be eaten by them. It's our whole life. So don't let it bother you."

The fish that uttered those words was caught up in the hands of a girl before it had even finished speaking, and soon its whole body was consumed.

So the carp disappeared, one after another, eaten by

people.

"What are you doing? Escape. Or you'll die too!"

They kept shouting at me to run away quickly, even while they were being devoured. For a moment I lost the power to escape, the shock of seeing the sticky-rice carp-cakes dying was so great. What could be the meaning of such short lives that ended in people's mouths as soon as they were born?

"Oh, this carp is a bit special. It'll be delicious."

A woman with red polish on her nails picked me up. She kept chewing and smacking her lips as if she cared nothing for the pain of the carp.

Just as the woman was about to put me into her mouth, I twitched my tail vigorously, went flying up, away from her and the brazier. She had certainly not been expecting me to go flying up into the sky, so she stared blankly after me with a shocked expression.

I kept flying up. A white cloud passed close above my head. Tears filled my eyes. I kept thinking of the sticky-rice carp-cakes, who never stopped shouting at me to get away quickly, even as they were dying.

Why had they kept shouting at me like that? What was the reason? Perhaps that too was love?

You must love right now. Do not put it off until tomorrow.

The sticky-rice carp-cakes must certainly have had that idea of love. If they had not loved me right then, on the spot, what would have become of me? I would probably have gone straight into that woman's mouth and died to the sound of her smacking lips.

Love is easy to talk about and sing about, but it is not easy to practice. But the carp had immediately loved me, even in their critical last moments.

Always love those you should love immediately. Do not put it off for tomorrow.

I flew on, reflecting on the lesson about life that the carp had given me.

Finally I emerged from Bundang. Highways stretched below me where cars sped along. Gradually darkness was spreading over the colt's-tail flowers and violets blooming on the ridges between the fields. How long had I been flying? At the foot of the hills, I saw a bright light beckoning to me.

I quickly flew in that direction. The light was coming from neon tubes decorating a signboard that read "Gonjiam Restaurant." One odd thing, however, was the fact that on the signboard was a carp, outlined in flickering lights. Beside the words "Steamed carp" and "Deep-fried carp," the carp formed of red lights kept flicking its tail up and down. My heart began to beat faster at the sight of it.

"If you're going to love, love right now."

I recalled the saying as I slowly approached the illuminated fish.

"You're really pretty. So bright. Quite dazzling. I've never seen a carp as beautiful as you."

As I approached, I confessed my feelings.

"I am Blue Bubble-Eyes. You have blue eyes, too. I think we might have met before, somewhere?"

Feeling increasingly love-struck, I moved in closer.

Suddenly he raised his tail and shouted coldly.

"Don't come any nearer. You mustn't come here. Go away quickly."

"Go away quickly? How can you say such a thing? Don't talk like that. Let's chat together."

I perched on the signboard and gazed at him with eyes full of affection.

"Go back where you came from, quickly, I tell you."

He looked at me with a pitying expression.

"This is a slaughterhouse for carp. It's a place where carp die gruesome deaths. So go back to wherever you came from quickly, before you're caught and killed."

I could not believe what he was saying. I wondered if he was saying things like that because he did not like me.

"Don't tell me lies. Let's talk. I've come all the way from Unjusa Temple in Hwasun to meet fish that attract me at first glance, like you."

"I'll tell you once more: get back home quickly. I don't love anyone. I'm not shining with neon for love. This world is too dangerous a place for carp. If you don't do as I say and something bad happens to you, don't blame me."

He was icy. He simply lowered his tail and refused even to look at me.

I did not want to leave there quickly. Perhaps because I had developed a crush on the brightly illuminated carp, I did not want to do something to make our meeting meaningless. No matter what dangers and trials might ensue, I felt sure I would to be able to cope with them.

I flew down from the signboard and cautiously glanced inside "Gonjiam Restaurant" through the partly open door. Inside the restaurant, a dozen or so people were enjoying dinner together in groups 'round the tables. Wherever I looked, the room was brightly lit; it did not look at all like a slaughterhouse for carp. There were several paintings on the walls, the painting of *The Angelus* by Millet particularly struck me. The picture of two peasants hearing the evening Angelus bell, bowing their heads and praying in an autumn field where harvest was over, touched me for some reason.

I was so taken with the picture that I did not realize at first that someone was holding me as hard as they could with both hands. By the time I realized that I had been caught by the restaurant owner, it was already too late to escape.

"Son of a bitch, what are you doing out here instead of being in the kitchen?"

To the sound of his cursing, I was carried into the kitchen and hurled into a large plastic bucket. I swooned. I bitterly regretted not having followed the advice of the illuminated carp. Without thinking, I screamed, "I'm not a fish, I'm a bird!" But no one was listening to me.

I heard the voice of the owner say, "You must keep the lid completely closed so that none of them can escape," then came the thud of the lid being closed.

It was completely dark inside the plastic bucket. I could not even try to fly. At the thought that my flying life was going to end here, I felt tears well up. The grieving face of Black Bubble-Eyes came into my mind, and the anxious faces of the recumbent Buddhas.

I had acted recklessly. I should have heeded the advice of the neon carp. I should have agreed that this world is too fearful and dangerous a place for carp.

I felt so reproachful toward myself that I could not stop crying.

"Don't cry too much."

Someone comforted me in a low voice. I finally lifted my head and looked around. The bucket was full of

95

carp caught before me. Dozens of carp, some bigger and some smaller than a human hand, were all gasping together. There were too many carp for the quantity of water; it was nothing less than a carp's idea of hell.

"I'm a carp who used to live in the Gonjiam reservoir. Don't cry too much. Crying won't help now. Our only task now is to comfort each other. We have to accept death while comforting one another. Everybody gets angry at first, refusing to accept it. They even start to blame God. And then slowly they come to accept the reality that they are going to die like this. Probably you will too."

I did not know how to reply. Reflect as I might, I felt so small that I just kept my mouth shut and blinked back my tears.

"Just think about the good things there have been. And those whom you have loved . . ."

The carp quietly came closer and patted my shoulder.

Well then, what had been the best thing in my life? Had saving the baby swallow and becoming able to fly been the best thing? Or had it been the first time I chimed and all the monks of Unjusa Temple came running out, exclaiming quietly? As for the one I had loved, I could not help remembering Black Bubble-Eyes. And the recumbent Buddhas who always taught me, and the white plover and the sticky-rice carp-cakes that gave their lives for me . . .

"And ask forgiveness of those we have wronged."

The carp kept patting my shoulder. His clear, white face loomed faintly through the darkness.

"It's not that I did not love you. I hated a life spent hanging there. Forgive me for leaving you."

Inwardly I begged Black Bubble-Eyes for forgiveness. Then my heart grew calmer. I began to think that if death could not be avoided, I could accept it now.

"So what happens next? What will become of me?"

I accepted death, but I was curious to know what would happen next. The thought that surely I couldn't just die like this made a sly appearance.

"You'll soon find out. Either you'll be fried in oil, or you'll have fiery spices spread over you then die slowly in a scalding cloud of steam. This restaurant specializes in carp. "

At last I understood the meaning of the words "Steamed carp" and "Deep-fried carp" on the neon signboard.

The lid of the bucket opened without warning. Abruptly, a hand holding a small net descended into the bucket and scooped up the carp I had been talking to.

"Bye! See you later in heaven!"

Before the carp had finished speaking, it had been dropped onto the kitchen table.

The cook did not close the lid of the bucket, and although I dared not try to escape, I poked my head out a little way and looked into the kitchen.

On the table, the carp was engaged in its last struggle. It repeatedly bent its body like a bow then straightened again.

Soon it could no longer do that.

The cook wrapped a cloth round the carp's head, sprinkled flour over its body, then pushed the floured part into a pan of seething oil.

Heavens!

I gaped in surprise, unable to close my mouth. Once the carp was in the oil, it began to fry with a sizzling sound.

As the illuminated carp on the signboard had said, it was truly a gruesome sight. It really was a slaughterhouse for carp.

The carp was soon fried a deep yellow. The cook took it out of the pan and untied the cloth wrapped around its head. The body was cooked, while the head was intact, as it had been. Its eyes were looking at me as if it was still alive.

I was in tears. I could not go on watching while the chef put the fish onto a large floral-pattern dish and sent it in to the customers.

I had been painfully holding my head above the water but now I pulled it back into the bucket. I had no further thought of living. Once I had seen one or two more carp die like the first, I did not even have a will to live. I would die like them if that was how I was meant to die. I had dreamed of a life on the wing, but if the result of the dream was to this degree empty of meaning, I had no choice but to accept it.

I waited for my turn to die at the cook's hands.

Soon it came.

This time, it was the owner's wife who, after taking the customers' order, dipped the net into the bucket. I made no attempt to avoid being caught.

"The customer on table 9 asked for a nice fresh one, so let's see whether this one is good or not."

The owner's wife repeated the customer's request

as she examined me carefully, then she began to look bewildered.

"Hey, why does this carp have such big fins?"

She turned the net this way and that, all the time staring at me.

"Hey, those aren't fins at all, they're wings, surely? A winged fish? Heavens! I've been running this restaurant for over ten years now, but this is the first time I've seen a fish like this. Honey, come and look here, honey! "

She made a great fuss as if something extraordinary had happened, as she called to her husband.

The owner, who had been helping the cook in the kitchen, thought there must be a fire and came rushing in.

"What's the matter? What's up?"

"Honey, look at this. These are not fins but wings, wings!"

"Wings? A carp with wings?"

"Yes. Look here. It's got wings."

She unfolded my wings fully. The owner fingered my wings suspiciously, then began to jump for joy as though he had won a lottery.

"Hey, this must be some kind of mutant. I've heard

of a farm where a white calf was born and the people made a fortune. Now I can earn a fortune with my winged carp. It looks as though this is my lucky year, and I'm going to move ahead."

The owner was so happy that he let the cigarette he was smoking go out half way through without noticing.

"We must sell this carp for a really high price. Ten times the normal price? No, I have to get at least 20 times more, even 100 times. Otherwise, why catch it? Why offer it to the customers?"

The owner's mouth was watering at the thought of earning some money and he spoke excitedly.

"Honey, you know Chairman Park of the South Seoul Golf Club, don't you? Give him a call. Tell him I have something special that's really good for stamina. The very best for stamina."

The owner went on and on chattering, while his wife remained much calmer. She looked at me for a long time as if she was thinking about something, then slowly began to speak.

"Honey, rather than that, why not let customers see it? If the rumor circulates among them that we have something rare to show them, they'll all come to see it.

Then naturally sales will go up."

"Nonsense. Suppose it dies, we'll be back where we started. You have to act while a creature like this is still alive. Are you new to this business?"

The owner was adamant. I suppose his argument that I should be sold for a high price while I was alive might probably have been right. However, the woman looked at me again more closely, as if a thought had struck her, then suddenly began to look nervous.

"Honey, let's not do that. We should let this carp go on living."

"Never! Why? What are you talking about?"

"Well, this is what I think. I think that if this carp gets killed and eaten, we'll be punished. You say it's good luck, but it's not. I reckon it's bad luck."

"Nonsense, I say. Don't waste your breath!"

"No. I'm right. This carp has magic powers. I can feel a kind of energy. There's no knowing what will happen to us if we kill this carp."

"What will happen to us? Something magic about this carp? If we sell it for a very high price, that's the end of it."

I could only listen in silence to the conversation between husband and wife. My fate depended on the outcome, but I felt as though I was listening to a conversation about someone else's fate.

"Honey, tomorrow is Buddha's Birthday, so let's spare this carp's life to mark that, and so make atonement for all the carp we've killed in the past."

"No. We'll earn a lot of money for it. Don't say that."

"Honey, if you go to the slaughterhouse, there's a memorial stone dedicated to the souls of the animals killed there. Once a year offerings are made in front of it for all the cattle that have died. And that's not all. If you go to the factory that weaves silk thread, there's monument to comfort the souls of the silkworms. There too people make offerings once a year for the dead silkworms. We don't make offerings for the dead carp but at least we should save this winged carp. It may be that heaven has sent it, to test us, I mean. When you come to think about it, how grateful we should be to the carp that feed our family day after day."

The owner curled his lips as though there was something more he wanted to say, but he made no reply. Perhaps reckoning she might be right, he lit up another cigarette before he spoke

"Oh, okay, okay. Do as you like. Fry it or spare it, you decide."

Finally, the owner was overruled by his wife.

Thanks to her, on the following morning I was taken out to the Buddha's Birthday ceremony of releasing captive animals on the shore of the Namhangang River at Yeoju and set free.

In the river I felt much cozier than in the air. Once my wings had appeared, I had quite forgotten that I was a fish that lives in the water, and the river felt correspondingly homely.

I threaded my way between the water weeds and roamed the open river. I could see plastic water bottles or soft drink cans floating among the reeds but paid no attention to them. It was not only life on the wing that was worth living; life swimming in the water also had its value.

"Go far away and live happily for a long, long time. Don't let yourself get caught again."

As I pondered the words the woman from the restaurant had spoken as she released me, I felt truly grateful to her. At the same time, I was grateful to God for letting me experience the pains of death. God had given me that pain because he loved me so, and as I swam along I reflected that when I suffered, God suffered with me.

The river continued to feel warm and cozy. Then someone came up behind me and tapped on my tail. Wondering who it might be, I stopped swimming and looked back. I saw a group of terrapins and turtles who had been released along with me at the riverside near Silleuksa Temple.

"Hello, Carp, let's go together."

They came hurrying after me, but they were so small. Some were only the size of a human little finger.

I played with them as we followed the river, at times in the lead, at times following them. But it was really odd. When the sun shone brightly through the water, I could see strange words written on them, such as "May our wishes be granted," "Success in exams," "Korean Unification," or "Park Sun-ja." The ugly inscriptions were written with black markers. But the terrapins and baby turtles frolicked in the river as if the words were of no importance.

"My goodness, humans . . ."

I spat out my scorn of humans without thinking. They say that if one dog barks at something, a hundred dogs follow suit and bark; that was how today's humans seemed.

I followed the stream and reflected that I had no wish to be one dog, let alone a hundred. As far as possible, I floated down the center of the river. I wanted to go somewhere far, far away, as the woman had said.

As I floated down the river, spring was coming to an end and summer was approaching. For over a month, it had not rained, the sun shone hot. The river was scorchingly hot, and the hotter it was the shallower it became. I sank ever deeper toward the riverbed as I floated on.

I lost count of time.

I suddenly realized that I was not being carried forward, I was stationary. I slowly put my head out of the water. I was no longer in a place where the river flowed onward, but in a reservoir into which the river flowed then stopped. Without realizing it, I had moved away from the center of the main river and followed a side-stream that fed into a reservoir.

At the foot of the rugged dike, reeds grew lush. The evening sun was dazzling as it set between the reeds. But at the foot of the reeds, trash lay dumped all over. There was a warning sign saying "Take your trash home" and "Whoever dumps trash here is liable to severe punishment." However, trash bags were piled up beneath the sign. It was not just garbage. A few broken TVs also lay abandoned. Some of the screens still seemed to be intact.

I raised my head above the surface of the water. I felt refreshed by the cool breeze. The green rice shoots that had begun to grow in the distant paddy fields shone red in the evening sunlight. The stout calves of the farmers who were heading home with shovels on their shoulders after taking care of the irrigation sluices looked beautiful. Here and there empty houses that people had abandoned were also visible.

I decided to continue my life in this reservoir for the time being. With that, I felt more fondly toward the surrounding landscape and I grew curious about the name of the reservoir.

"What's the name of this reservoir?" I asked a carp who like me had its head out of the water and was looking at the evening scene.

"Hupo Reservoir. The water's deep here and there's plenty of mud and a lot of water-weed, so it's a good place for us carp to live. But the problem is that recently, many anglers have begun coming here. We have to be on the alert. You should be careful."

He was as tender and caring as Black Bubble-Eyes. For a moment I mistook him for Black Bubble-Eyes and was about to hug him.

"Anglers? What are anglers?"

The word "angler" was very unfamiliar.

"They are the people who catch us. They are all the time deceiving us and we are all the time foolishly falling victim to them. Especially those of us who are careless take a bite of bait suspended from fishing hooks, are snared, and as their mouths tear, their carefree youth ends. Yesterday I lost my youngest son. Even though I took such care of him, he swallowed the bait. I've been so sad and upset, but now my tears have dried."

The carp who claimed his tears had dried was unable to go on talking and shed more bitter tears. I wiped away the tears from his eyes.

"Thanks. You are very kind. But do be careful. Otherwise, you'll not survive. If only there were no anglers, this place would be a paradise for us."

Everywhere, life was at risk. But I had no intention of leaving Hupo Reservoir. Above all, I liked it because so many carp lived there, so I would not be lonely. Perhaps it would be the place where I could meet my true life's partner.

That night, the carp who had lost his son introduced me to the other fish as a carp from the Namhangang River. They merely thought I had fins rather bigger than those of other carp, and could not even imagine in their wildest dreams that I was a carp with wings.

That night, as the hours passed, they told me some rules, taboos that I must observe as a carp living in the reservoir.

First, do not be curious about the world outside the water.

Second, do not trust any human, even a child, and never go close to them.

Third, think that any food that humans offer is sure to be bait and do not eat it. In particular, do not eat the freshwater worms that we most enjoy eating. Above all, rid yourself of gluttony.

Fourth, do not neglect to study the difference between fishing boats and barges, fishing lines and grass stalks, lead weights and pebbles.

Fifth, do not fall in love with someone else's sweetheart.

There were a few other taboos, such as "Do not be attracted by bright lights," but I did not bother listening to them all because I reckoned I could keep almost all of them except the first.

On the surface, the days at Hupo were peaceful. When the sun rose in the morning, sunlight glittered on the surface of the water, a breeze that shook the reeds was always blowing, and at night the starlight was also bright and peaceful.

But where in the world can there be true peace?

Seen from outside, the reservoir might seem peaceful but beneath the water the sound of wailing never ceased. When the anglers came roaring up in vans and plied their fishing poles all night long, in the morning they took away with them dozens of carp they had caught overnight. No matter how much the older carp urged the younger ones to keep the rules, they paid no heed. Occasionally even old carp were caught, perhaps having grown senile, and they paid the price of celebrity, being hailed as "big fish."

The anglers were cunning. They invariably only prepared food that the carp liked, so that the fish could not resist eating their bait. Even though they knew that eating meant certain death, they could not resist, and were all the time being caught.

Only the carp that knew how to hold firm survived. Those lacking patience disappeared one by one. The sound of wailing never ceased. Funeral services held in the absence of a body were a daily occurrence. Planning committee meetings were held every night to discuss how they might prevent the anglers from coming, but the only way seemed to be for the carp to be careful not to let themselves be caught. As the anglers said, if the fishing was bad, people would naturally stop coming, but the fish were stupid.

I was deeply troubled. I could not simply go somewhere else on my own, leaving them alone. I spent every night wondering how I could bring an end to their tears but found no solution. I felt depressed. I lost my appetite. My sole pleasure lay in nibbling a few sunbeams on the surface of the water in the mornings.

Then, one such morning, after the night's anglers had already set off for home, I set out in search of some sunbeams to eat. I spotted a silvery scrap of sunlight shining, dazzlingly bright, below the surface of the water on the eastern side, where an empty farmhouse was reflected. I bit into the sunshine without further thought. I did not for one moment suspect that the sunshine was connected to a fishhook.

Oh, I had been wrong. I thought all the anglers had gone home, but some had stayed behind, and the sunshine was being reflected from one of their hooks.

As I swallowed the sunshine, I felt something hard catch in my throat, causing a sharp pain.

I resisted with all my might, but I was being pulled along at the end of a taut fishing line. Then I found myself out of the water, flapping in the air. "Wow, it's a big one!" If it had not been for the cheers of human onlookers, I might have imagined that I had begun to fly again.

I felt my mouth being torn by the hook. It was so painful that I thought I was going to pass out, but I could not make a sound.

The man who had caught me began by bringing out his camera, smiling brightly.

"Okay, take some good shots. This month's prize for the biggest catch is mine for sure."

The man reeled in the line, clutched it firmly, and climbed up the reservoir embankment.

"Now, snap away. Hey, Hu-min, come here, let's have you in the picture too."

The man lifted me up to the level of his eyes, still keeping his satisfied smile.

I was a sorry sight, with the fishing line caught in my mouth, my tail dangling and my head pointing straight up at the sky.

The man began to wash me with salt water, saying he first of all wanted to sap my energy. After soaking the towel in salt water he slowly washed me thoroughly. He did not seem to be worried whether any of my scales might drop off. However, as the man opened wide my wings, which had shrunk to the size of fins, and began to wash them carefully, he mumbled to himself as if there was something suspicious.

"Isn't this a carp? It's weird. The fins look like wings. Hey, Kim, aren't these wings?" The man, who had only been blinded by my size and had not realized that I was a flying fish, shouted at Mr. Kim.

"Hey, you're in big trouble. It's a flying fish. You're right about the wings."

Kim recognized what I was right away.

"A flying fish?"

"Yes, man, it's a flying fish I tell you!"

"A flying fish . . ."

The man pushed Kim aside, examined my wings, and then smiled as he muttered.

"Wow, I'm really in luck. This means not only the prize for the biggest fish but the special species prize as well . . ."

"Hey, man, what are you talking about? You'd better release it fast. Otherwise you'll be in even worse trouble."

I was caught and dying, yet it looked as though I was really scaring Kim intensely. But the man who had caught me was not reacting in the same way.

"Trouble? What trouble? Rather, it's great! I have to make a print of this rare species to show posterity."

"No, you're wrong. There are things that are taboo to us anglers. When I was still only a kid I heard from my grandfather that if you catch a flying fish it must be released unharmed. A friend of my grandfather's once caught a flying fish that he cooked and ate instead of letting it live. As a consequence he was cursed and several members of his family died in quick succession. So listen, man, you have to be careful. The fact that a carp has been given wings to fly through the heavens is the clearest evidence that the heavens have

115

come down to earth."

Kim continued to insist that I should be saved, even invoking ancestral history. However, his arguments were in the end of no avail in the face of the man's stubbornness.

After pulling the hook out of my mouth he smeared my whole body up to my eyes with ink. The morning sunlight was still dazzling. Death seemed to be approaching rapidly. I longed to feed on sunlight one last time so I opened my mouth as wide as I could.

The man doused the cotton balls liberally with ink and carefully applied it to my body. I was soon completely covered with black ink. The poison in the ink permeated my skin, heating my body until I could hardly breathe. Naturally, I was unable to open my eyes. By the time the man rubbed the ink over my wings and tail, I was almost dead.

When I felt my body being covered with rice paper, I could only remain immobile. The man's hands moved nimbly and delicately, pressing the paper down. Intent on ensuring that the paper was well permeated with the ink, he did not neglect the smallest corner.

"Good, good. It's come out really well. It's the best print I've ever made."

The man laughed again, a satisfied laugh.

"Now, I'm hungry. Let's all go and have some break-fast."

The man set off, leading the whole group to the restaurant at the entrance of the reservoir, and I was left lying on the grass, waiting for the moment of death to come.

Just then a boy approached me and wiped the blood from my mouth. It was that same Hu-min.

"I'm sorry, flying fish. Come on, now, fly, won't you?"

The boy wanted me to go flying away. But I could not fly. My whole body felt so weak that I could not so much as move.

"I really do want to see you go flying. Fly, won't you, please?"

The boy filled a bucket with water and laid me in it. At last I began to come to my senses. I reckoned that if the boy wanted to see me flying through the air, I should not disappoint him. I braced myself. Slowly I moved my wings. Suddenly I was flying again. It was a miracle!

The boy waved goodbye. I left the reservoir behind after circling twice above the boy's head as a sign of gratitude.

I did not cry. I could only give thanks. How grateful I felt on having been saved from the brink of death. Moreover, how grateful I felt that just then a brief shower came and washed the remaining traces of ink from my body.

In the past, I did not know how to be grateful. I did not realize that the fact of being alive was something I should always be thankful for. Truly, I ought to have felt grateful when I was living a fulfilled life, and foolishly I had not. Now I was so glad and thankful to be alive after suffering the pains of death several times.

Still feeling grateful, I longed to find a place where

I could just rest quietly. I was scared and appalled at the thought of ever going back to the human world. I passed over rice fields and meadows, passed over plains, and flew energetically toward the mountains that rose at the far end of the plains.

I went flying on and on.

Just at sunset, I glimpsed an empty, abandoned house at the foot of Myeongjisan Mountain in Gapyeong. I did not hesitate but went flying toward the house. The grass was tall in the yard but I liked it because a crape myrtle was blooming there. The water in the well had not yet dried up, and on the storage terrace, broken crocks lay, half-full of rainwater. In the backyard some small farming tools such as picks and hoes remained lying about, too.

There were some household articles inside the room, including a brush made of twigs and a dustpan, and a bamboo hook of the kind people use to scratch their back when it itches. I was amused to see a brass chamber pot lying in a corner of the bedroom. There was an overcoat hanging on a clothes rack, and a picture of a young man wearing a graduation cap on the wall. Near it there hung a wedding photograph with a bride and groom in a wedding hall along with the officiant. Maybe it was the wedding of that same young man. And beside it, there hung another picture, perhaps of someone's sixtieth birthday party, where an elderly couple were sitting in the center behind a ceremonially decorated table with various descendants around them.

They looked so harmonious that I stayed looking at the photos for quite a while. I suddenly found myself thinking of Black Bubble-Eyes. I was thinking that, like that elderly couple in the photo, I wanted to live for a long time in this empty house with Black Bubble-Eyes and have babies together. But that thought soon faded. It was nothing but a futile dream to imagine bringing Black Bubble-Eyes flying here to live with me, when all he wanted was to live hanging forever from the temple roof.

The twilight glow faded and night soon came. Fireflies emerged, the moon shone bright. It was not yet autumn yet the grasshoppers were chirping loudly. The moonlight glimmered in the water held in the broken crocks on the terrace. I immersed myself in the water and lay there for a long time.

One day passed, then two. Ten days passed, then a month passed. Early autumn passed, then it was late autumn. The leaves began to fall and chill winds blew. The fruit on the persimmon tree beside the well began to ripen red. Sometimes birds came flying to peck at them. A few people arrived in the paddy fields one morning, cut the rice with sickles and left it lying there. An elderly woman with a bent back, accompanied by her grandchild, spread red peppers in the front yard to dry. I leaped out of the water and flew to the tip of a persimmon tree branch.

"I am not a fish. I don't want to live in water any longer." I shouted at myself.

I no longer wanted to live the life of a fish. Just as the boy who had saved me wanted to see me flying in the sky as a bird, I too wanted to see myself more as a bird.

"Anything with wings is a bird. I am now a bird, not a fish."

I thought of myself in that manner and went flying up into the sky like a bird.

Body and mind feel equally light. The sky may be the same sky, yet there is still a great difference between flying in the sky thinking I'm a fish and flying in the sky thinking I'm a bird. The world seen from inside a broken crock and the world seen while flying through the blue sky feel very different.

When your mind changes, your behavior changes, and when your behavior changes, life feels different. Let's go flying. In order not to waste this one day of life called today, let's go flying. In order never to forget that the day I waste today is the tomorrow the plover and carp who died yesterday so longed to see, let's go flying. Let's become birds and go flying. No one can gain a life of true freedom without some suffering, surely?

I flew on for several days and nights. By day, I received strength from the grass swaying in the wind, and by night I received strength from the Morning Star, which rises the earliest and sets the latest. When darkness grew deep, the stars were sure to shine. When night was over, morning was sure to come. And once morning came, the world grew dazzling with sunlight.

One day, a subway station came looming between the sunbeams. I came to earth gently near the entrance. On the signboard I read "Moran." I was back in Seongnam city in Gyeonggi-do Province, where I had met the sticky-rice carp-cakes.

The neighborhood around Moran Station was crowded and noisy. In front of the intercity bus terminal, one middle-aged man with a loudspeaker kept shouting at people to believe in Jesus. The man did not seem to know that sometimes a whisper moves the human heart better than oratory can, the soft chime of a wind-bell rather than the noise of a piano.

I went on past the terminal and headed for Moran Market. Today being the fifth day, it was market day, and the place was swarming with people. Most of the merchants were street vendors, selling underwear or socks piled on their carts; others were selling glutinous rice, sorghum, millet, and buckwheat, various kinds of cereals. There was even a man with a stall on which the corpses of dead dogs, singed black, were exposed for sale.

The dead dogs looked so pitiful that I could not tear myself away. I watched the dog-meat butcher for a while, as he busily touted his wares: "If you like what you see, better buy it at once." And I prayed for the souls of the dead dogs. Since they say short prayers reach heaven soonest, I offered the shortest possible prayer, then left.

The entrance to Moran Station was still crowded with people. Having no desire to fly off somewhere else, I sat on the station name board and watched the people coming and going. People walked so fast that it seemed as if life was an immensely busy affair. It was hard to find anyone walking slowly. I muttered to myself at the sight of people hastily vanishing down underpass steps, along narrow alleys, or boarding buses: "Everyone seems to be rushing off somewhere."

Just then a bird settled beside me and on overhearing my words said, "Everyone's going home. Just as we have nests, people all have houses." It was a very small bird, the size of a child's fist. I felt most grateful that it had recognized me as a bird.

"Who are you?"

"I'm a finch."

He smiled at me with small, blinking eyes. I was about to say "I'm a flying fish," but quickly stopped myself, wondering what would be the bird's reaction if it learned that I was really a fish.

"Where are you going?"

If ever he said he was going to Seoul, I might have offered to accompany him. However, the finch said he had never been to Seoul, having been born and always lived in Moran.

"I tell fortunes in Moran. I'm a fortune-telling bird."

"Fortune telling? What's that?"

It was the first time I had ever heard the expression.

"It means predicting and telling people about their fate. Everyone wants to know in advance what their fortune is. They want to avoid bad things, and if good things are coming, they want to wait hopefully for them, and I help them find out what's coming. It's sometimes called ornithomancy, because it's a bird that does the fortune-telling."

I felt very curious about this fortune-telling. Seeing my curiosity, the finch invited me to follow him.

The place where we landed was across the street, near the signboard of Moran Station. An elderly man wearing an old fedora was sitting on the cold sidewalk with a small cage, the door of which was open. Next to the cage, a sheet of cardboard was propped, with the words "Bird fortune telling 1,000 won" written on it.

"Hello, Grandpa, how are you?"

The finch greeted the old man and flew into the cage. Then the old man closed the cage door and began to wait for people to come to have their fortunes told by the bird.

Soon people started to gather.

"What's this?"

Some were amazed and had their fortune told, others just stayed squatting next to the cage and watched what happened.

I flew back up onto the subway sign and watched the scene.

As the sun set and passers-by grew rarer, the old man opened the cage door again.

"Bye, Grandpa."

The finch wished him good night and quickly flew up to my side.

"What do you think? Fun, isn't it?"

The finch patted my shoulder with a smile, as if boasting.

"I want to try, too. It looks like real fun. Couldn't I give it a try?"

"If you want to. I'll introduce you to grandfather."

I really wanted to tell fortunes. But I was afraid the old man might keep me shut up in the cage all the time. The finch assured me he would not.

"He won't. He doesn't keep me locked in. We've been telling fortunes with this old man for several generations. We have an agreement, a promise. I'm only shut up in the cage when I'm telling fortunes. Otherwise I'm free to fly about as I please. We've lived like that that since our ancestors' times, and the promise has always been kept. So far it's never been broken. We trust each other. That's the most important thing. Without trust, all relationships are sure to break down."

That night. I followed the finch to the nearby mountain fortress of Namhansanseong and slept in the woods there. We returned to Moran Station about one o'clock the next day.

The old man was already waiting with the cage in front of the station.

"Grandpa, this is my friend."

The finch introduced me to the old man.

"My friend wants to try telling fortunes."

The old man stared at me. His gaze was like that of the recumbent Buddha, so I felt at ease.

"Very well, if that's what you want. It'll be better if you have a friend. Nothing is worse than not having a friend in the world, having no one to whom you can open your heart."

As soon as he gave his permission, I entered the cage with the finch and we began to take turns telling fortunes.

It was not very difficult. There was a partition made of bamboo in the middle of the cage. On one side of it the finch waited, on the other side there was a small wooden box holding tightly packed folded slips of paper on which people's fortunes were written. When the old man opened the partition, he walked to the side with the wooden box and picked out with his beak whichever slip of paper he felt moved to choose. Then the old man took the paper and gave it to the person who had paid and was waiting.

The expressions on the faces of people as they received the paper with their fortune were various. While some people frowned seriously, wrinkling their foreheads, others smiled broadly as if hearing good news. I think most of the papers indicated good luck. For example, "At twenty-seven you will meet someone high-up and receive an unexpected proposal. The course of your life may change, so reflect well before deciding."

I enjoyed fortune-telling. I had the impression I was becoming involved in people's destinies, that I was doing something significant. Besides, I was not lonely. Both the finch and the old man were extremely kind. At the end of the day, when our work was done, he would be sure to open the door and set us free. Not only that, he always gave us plenty of good food. The different kinds of millet were delicious, and sometimes he bought sugar-filled pancakes from which he broke little pieces to give to us, and they were so tasty that I ate a lot. Once night fell, we went back to sleep in the pine forests of Namhansanseong, which was a good place to live. There, beautiful, centuries-old pine trees covered the mountain, so that it felt cozy like the mountain ridge of Unjusa Temple. And best of all, once I began to tell fortunes, the old man's income more than doubled.

"Is that a bird or a fish? It looks as though it might have magic power."

Making remarks of that kind, people showed more interest in me than in the finch.

Finally a rumor spread that I had miraculous powers of fortune-telling, and crowds came thronging to Moran Station to have their fortunes told. Sometimes there was a really long queue in front of the cage.

Among all the people coming, I felt happiest on seeing children who came with their mothers. The eyes of the children looking at me were so bright. When I saw their gaze, I forgot all the pain I had suffered.

All that while, time was passing. Fallen leaves piled up in the streets, then if even a slightly strong wind blew, the fallen leaves vanished somewhere down the alleys. When news of the first frost and the first ice at Daegwallyeong Pass spread, people began to hunch their shoulders and bring out their winter clothes.

The old man often coughed. As the days passed he declined visibly, like the falling leaves. There were people who urged him not to work on the street in the cold wind but to rent a room somewhere and take some time off to rest, too, but he insisted on coming out to the street regularly.

"If I don't do it, this kind of fortune-telling may vanish completely. Maybe I'm the last in this world to do it."

The old man was afraid that the art of fortune-telling with birds might vanish forever from this planet. And finally that was what happened.

It was another day with a bitter wind blowing. The finch and I headed for Moran Station where the old man was always stationed. But there was no sign of him, although he invariably arrived before us. We waited for one hour, two hours, and still he did not come.

"This has never happened before . . . What can be the matter?"

The finch was so worried that he could not remain still for a second but kept flying here and there around the streets near the station. I thought he might be having some pancakes or fishcakes to eat and searched along every alley. But there was no trace of the old man. Darkness spread over the streets, night came, and still he did not appear.

"That's enough. Let's go to Grandpa's house. I've

been there once," the finch said in an urgent voice.

I followed him into the darkness as we flew through the night sky.

The house was very high up, in a so-called "moon-village" shanty-town.

"There's the house."

Hanging in front of the gate of the simple house, which the finch pointed to, there was a red paper lantern with two black characters written on it. I did not know what the lantern meant, but as soon as he saw the lantern, the finch understood that the old man had passed away.

"Oh, Grandad has died!"

Tears flowed from his eyes.

The old man had high blood pressure, and the previous night something had made him angry so he drank rather more than usual before he went to sleep. Then in the morning they had found him dead.

I was sad. Like the finch, tears flowed from my eyes. I recalled the recumbent Buddha's saying that death was like the waves of the sea. But the fact that there was now no one in the world who knew how to tell fortunes using birds was really sad.

The waning moon was gazing down at me silently

from the night sky. The stars were shining, whether or not they knew how I was feeling.

I could tell that the time had come for me to leave Moran. There was no need for me to stay now that I could no longer tell fortunes. The finch suggested we might live together in the Namhansanseong pine forest, but I did not want to.

"Goodbye, finch. Thanks for everything."

That night I parted from the finch. I felt sorry to leave him, but it did not hurt. Although we had been affectionately close, it was not love, so it was not so painful.

The first snow was falling. I flew toward Seoul amid the snowflakes. On the day I had my first glimpse of snow at Unjusa Temple, Black Bubble-Eyes and I had eaten our fill of it. I ate so much of the first snow that the next day my droppings were all white. I had glimpsed husband and wife recumbent Buddhas throwing snowballs at each other, then go strolling along the snowy paths holding hands.

I flew toward Seoul, all the while eating the fresh snow, as on that day.

Seoul was beautiful, buried in white snow. The first snow was falling in order to make Seoul beautiful. The first snow made all the trees, grass, mice, even the people in Seoul beautiful.

I went first to the Insa-dong Buddhist store and from there to Seoul Station. I had the feeling that if I went to Seoul Station, the direction I should head in would be decided. The station is the way and also the beginning of the way, so I wanted to find my way again at Seoul Station.

The station was dressed in white. The first snowfall was a true blizzard. I perched on the clock tower in the station square and watched the passers-by. The people walking through the falling snow were beautiful. Even the homeless no longer looked poor. A young mother walking over the snowy paths holding her young daughter's hand was more beautiful than anyone else in the world.

The snow stopped and suddenly it was late at night. All the trains arriving from the south under the snow had set off for Susaek, and only homeless people lingered near the waiting room at Seoul Station.

The thought suddenly came to me that Black Bubble-Eyes might be hanging around nearby, and I kept an eye on the street below. Then I began to count the footprints in the square. Try as I might, I could not

count the number. It was as hard and tiring as counting the number of stars in the night sky.

The hand of the clock tower was pointing to two o'clock in the morning. The crescent moon was floating white over the dome of Seoul Station. I gave up counting the footprints and flew up onto the dome to sleep.

"Why? Who is this? Aren't you the flying fish?"

Someone saw me and shouted with pleasure. It was a gray pigeon. It was the very same gray pigeon that had so warmly comforted me when I first came to Seoul and was sleeping under the bridge.

He turned his back on the moon, came waddling toward me, and embraced me firmly. I did not resist his embrace. I briefly felt that it must be fate that enabled me to meet him again in this scary and lonely Seoul, after I had completely forgotten about him.

"What are you doing here? Why are you sleeping here and not at City Hall?"

I wondered why he was sleeping on the dome of Seoul Station.

"I was kicked out by the City Hall pigeons. A person with any kind of disability is not allowed to live on the roof of City Hall. They reckon it defiles the honor of

Seoul. So I made my home on this dome where no one is looking at me. This time, one of my left toes is gone, you see."

While we were separated, he had lost another toe, and he looked pitiful.

"I'm sorry. It must have hurt a lot."

This time it was I who hugged him.

"No it's okay. Wow . . . I never expected to see you again. I'm really glad."

He was overjoyed and would not leave my side for a moment. That night I slept with the gray pigeon. We slept embracing one another warmly. Before we fell asleep we exchanged a gentle kiss. I'm not a fish, I'm a bird. As we kissed I reminded myself once again that I was thinking of myself as a bird. Because I thought I was a bird, I did not consider it ethically wrong to share love with a pigeon.

The next morning, unexpectedly, I felt sick and could not move. The sun that was melting the snow shone down brightly on the world, but I lay prostrate on the dome. Perhaps it was because I had been having so hard a life. I grew increasingly feverish and began to shiver.

"This is serious."

The gray pigeon looked at me anxiously before flying down onto the street to collect some snow with which to cool my body. Next he found scraps of ice to rub me with. I did not feel like eating, but he brought back some cookie crumbs which he kept putting into my mouth.

I suffered from high fever for three days and nights. The gray pigeon nursed me throughout those three days and nights, hardly sleeping at all. If I asked him for some more snow, he stopped whatever he was doing to go and fetch snow and ice chips. Thanks to the pigeon's devotion, after three days the dreaded high fever gradually began to abate. And a week later, I had recovered fully.

"Thank you. Without you, I would have died."

I gratefully kissed the back of the gray pigeon's claw.

"Nonsense . . . I did what had to be done, that's all."

The gray pigeon was very humble and rejoiced that I had regained my health as though it had happened to him.

Without even talking about it, we naturally began to live together on the green dome of Seoul Station. Neither of us said "I love you," but we each knew that we loved each other. The pigeon had moved to Seoul

Station in order to meet me, and if I had left Unjusa Temple, it had surely been in order to meet the pigeon.

Every day, everything felt new. Every morning the sunshine was brighter and warmer, Seoul Station grew ever more beautiful. The Daewoo Building and Namsan Tower over across the street seemed more beautiful. On days when we went flying together as far as the Hangang Railway Bridge, the 63 Building, even all the way to far-off Haengjusanseong Fortress or Bukhansan Mountain, on our return I would massage his legs lovingly. Nothing made me happier than thinking what I could do for the gray pigeon.

"Love right now. Do not put it off for tomorrow."

I had never forgotten those words. Every night, I fell asleep telling myself that I loved him. I fell asleep, giving thanks that at last I was not living in vain.

But alas, such days were not to last much longer.

On that fateful day gloomy sleet was falling over Seoul. A silver dove came flying to the dome of Seoul Station in search of the gray pigeon. The silver dove was living in Deoksugung Palace and was already very close to the gray pigeon.

"Do you realize how long I've been looking for you? Why did you go away without saying anything? If you

were kicked out of Seoul City Hall, you could have come to Deoksugung Palace, couldn't you?"

"I'm sorry. In Deoksugung Palace I would have been meeting the city hall pigeons all the time. So I decided to go somewhere farther away."

The gray pigeon did not really apologize to the silver dove but from that day on the silver dove never left the gray pigeon's side. The silver dove spent the nights on the antique bronze dome of Seoul Station then spent the days there. I did not want to welcome the silver dove. She was an intruder who had invaded my love nest.

"Gray pigeon! I dislike sharing you with that silver dove. I want to be alone with you."

I told him many times that I wanted to live alone with him, but the gray pigeon pretended not to hear. Then, after a while, he made it clear that he wanted to live alone with the silver dove.

I was upset. I found it hard to understand what the gray pigeon's attitude meant. However, I reckoned that if that was what he wanted, I ought not to stand in his way. That was because I loved him.

At first, once it was plain that the gray pigeon was living with the silver dove, he adopted an extremely apologetic attitude toward me. However, as time passed, he made it increasingly plain that he considered it natural for them to live like that.

Claiming that his legs were aching, he entrusted the collection of food to me entirely, and would not let me stay sitting on the dome for more than ten minutes at a time.

"What will we do if you bring back so little food? You have to bring back enough for the silver dove as well, remember."

He became more and more demanding. He refused to sleep with me and always slept hugging the silver dove, then woke up late in the morning. He did not give a damn for the saying that the early bird gets the worm.

I was kept busy collecting enough food for the silver dove to have her share. I went flying from one side of Seoul Station to the other, from Malli-dong to Gong-deok-dong, collecting food that people had discarded. Of course, I only gave them the most delicious and cleanest morsels. On days when I could not find much food, I fasted.

However, there was no end to the gray pigeon's demands.

"Why is your skin so rough? I hate scales. They're hard. I could put up with you if your skin were as soft as the silver dove's."

He was right. To become a bird I had to get rid of my scales. I had not realized that. So long as I have scales on my body, I am not a bird.

I removed the scales for love's sake. Enduring the

pain, shedding blood, I ripped off my scales one by one. If the wind blew even a little or if I struck something, I would feel cold or develop a scar, but so long as it was what the one I loved wanted I could bear that much pain.

"Hey, look. I got rid of the scales you didn't like. I'm soft now."

I showed the gray pigeon my skin. He merely burst out laughing as if I were being absurd.

"It's not just the scales. It's everything about you. Those bulging blue eyes, that soft, baggy skin on your belly, that revolting, slimy tail. What about all that?"

I stared at him blankly, completely at a loss for words.

"I'm telling you plainly: you're not a bird, you're a fish. I can't share love with a fish. I can't love a fish. I used to have dust in my eyes, I was blind. I'm sorry I ever met you. I want to forget the days I spent with you. Go on, get away from here. No, okay, I'm leaving. I'm off to Namsan Tower to live. There I'll be looking down on Seoul from somewhere higher than you. Goodbye! Farewell! Goddamn fish!"

So the gray pigeon left me and went off with the silver dove.

I cried. Seoul Station was wet with my tears. People

passing beside Seoul Station stopped at the sound of my crying and looked up at the dome.

Sleet was falling intermittently. Above all, I was troubled at how hard it was to control my anger. I did not know what to do about that anger.

I just kept gazing at the lights of the trains on their way to Susaek.

Time passed. Time gave birth to more time. Time gave birth to nothing but itself. Finally, one day I addressed the lights of a train headed for Susaek:

"I'm sorry to bother you, but could you summon the recumbent Buddha's starlight for me?"

Fortunately the lights did as I asked. That night, the Buddha's starlight came visiting me.

"Recumbent Buddha, I have been betrayed by love. More than anything else, I am suffering because I cannot overcome my anger."

At first, seeing the Buddha's starlight, I had wept.

"Don't cry. Don't hurt yourself because of your anger. What matters is that you loved him. For love, that fact alone is enough."

"But still the pain won't go away."

"There is no life without suffering. Don't hope for a life without pain. Pain is as normal as eating or sleeping."

"But why am I feeling such pain?"

"It is not only others who suffer pain. The only way to endure pain is to remember that I, too, may feel pain."

"My wound is deep."

"There is no beauty without wounds. The pearl has its wound, the petal has its wound. The beauty of the rose is the fruit of its wound."

"I have lost so much."

"But you have not yet lost everything. Take courage. Find out for yourself what you have not lost."

The Buddha's starlight disappeared.

Then I saw a black smoke of anger slowly ebbing away from my body.

There is no love without wounds. If the rose is beautiful, it's because of its wounds. I lost much but did not lose everything.

A full moon rose bright over the station's green dome. Recalling what the Buddha's starlight had said, I set off. The city was huge. I went flying low above it. Somewhere nearby I heard people singing. The streets and alleys around Gwanghwamun and along Jongno were full of the sound of Christmas carols.

Suddenly I missed the quiet chimes of the mountain temple's wind chimes. I longed to hear Black Bubble-Eyes's bell awakening from sleep the pine trees buried in snow, one after another. But I could not leave for Unjusa Temple right away like that.

After reflecting for a moment where I might be able to hear a wind chime in Seoul, I spread my wings energetically and headed for Jogyesa Temple. The temple was not far from Jonggak subway station. An icy winter wind was blowing from Bukhansan Mountain, and soon I could hear the sound of the wind chimes hanging from the eaves of the temple's main hall

I listened quietly. Perhaps because it was located in the very center of the city, surrounded with high-rise buildings, the sound of the wind chimes could not be compared with that I had heard at Unjusa Temple. But there was nothing in the least lacking to cool my heart, which had been burning with anger.

"Hello! I'm the fish from a wind chime at Unjusa Temple."

I greeted the fish of the wind chime of Jogyesa Temple as it shook in the wind.

"How did you come all this way? Oh, you've got wings!"

He was not really surprised by my wings. I thought he would raise his tail vigorously in astonishment, but that did not happen.

"I once had wings like you. I was a flying fish like you. Now the wings have quite atrophied, yet . . ."

"What? You say you were a flying fish?"

It was my turn to be surprised.

"Yes, back before. I thought that there must be a better life than hanging up here like this, so I became a flying fish and went flying through the air. Seeing you, I see myself as I was a few decades ago."

In my heart I heard the "Boom!" of a rock rolling downhill. I had never even dreamed that there could be another flying fish beside me, with the possible exception of Black Bubble-Eyes, perhaps.

"Why, your scales have all been torn off! You're really badly wounded. Doesn't it hurt? It looks as though you've been through some really hard times."

"I've been through so many hardships. I nearly died several times. And I experienced failure in love . . ."

"Ha ha, I knew it. But don't let it get you down too much. It's all about learning."

"It's already in the past. Where is there a life without suffering?"

"Indeed so . . . Everyone wants a life without pain, but that's the same as saying I will not eat even though I am hungry."

"But you are not a flying fish any more. Why are you back hanging up like this again?"

"Um, it's . . . because I was able to clearly understand the essence of my life."

He kept blinking as he spoke. He was a blue bubble-eyes like me.

"The essence of your life? But what is it?"

"It's not a life flying about like you, it's a life spent hanging up like this. Since I am a wind chime through and through, the essence of my life is to emit a clear, quiet wind-bell sound. For me, a life spent flying around, since then I cannot produce the ring of a wind chime, is a life divorced from its essence and therefore not really worth living. Because I am a fish, not a bird. It is futile for a fish to become a bird. At first it felt as though I was living a creative life, but I was not. I almost lost my existence. I was able to regain it by coming back to being a wind bell again. And thus I was able to realize the fundamental truth of my life."

He had put his finger on my life's central problem. He had discerned at a glance that I was thinking of myself as a bird, not a fish.

Struck by an unaccustomed diffidence, my voice failed me and I remained silent. Then he spoke again:

"I suppose it was because you are so exhausted that you wanted to come and hear the sound of a wind bell?"

"Yes, you're right. I'm exhausted. And I'm worried about how I should live in the future."

"That means that you are now ready to go back to Unjusa Temple. Go back quickly. Your partner must be waiting so impatiently for you to return. The fishes of wind bells that face each other under the same roof are lovers who once loved each other in a past life. That's why they face one another in this present life."

"Really?"

"Really. If it were not so, why would you miss the sound of the Unjusa Temple wind bells as you do?"

The cold wind from Bukhansan Mountain continued to blow. Being without scales, I had to keep flying here and there around the Jogyesa courtyards in order to keep warm. Occasionally I perched on the branches of the centuries-old spindle tree growing in front of the main hall and kept a lookout for the monk who had helped Black Bubble-Eyes and myself to live as wind bells in Unjusa Temple, in case he was still living here.

There was no sign of him. Instead of the monk, there were a few pots of winter poinsettias standing on the stone steps of the temple hall. There was a young artist drawing in a sketchbook a little way off, facing the steps. I looked over his shoulder at the picture he was drawing. Unexpectedly, he was drawing the Jogyesa wind bell. On the far left side of the page he had drawn the wind bell, with beyond it the eaves of the temple hall and a cold winter sky spread above it, where the dry branches of the tree extended.

I looked at the picture for a long time. Then I suddenly coughed loudly. Perhaps I had caught a cold. The painter glanced round at me, then looked surprised.

"Hey, excuse me, but are you by any chance from Unjusa Temple?"

I kept coughing and could not answer at once.

"Aren't you by any chance the fish from the wind bell at Unjusa Temple?"

The artist repeated his question and I stammered a reply.

"Yes, yes, but how do you know me?"

I was amazed that there might be someone in Seoul who would recognize me.

"Oh, so I was right after all. I was wondering . . . In that case, I've something to show you. Let's go to my studio."

Without waiting for my reply, the artist closed his sketchbook. I followed the car he was driving. His studio was on a hill looking toward Inwangsan Mountain. There was a big window in one wall, through which Inwangsan Mountain was plainly visible.

"Actually, I have a picture I want to show you."

The painter showed me two drawings of the main hall at Unjusa Temple.

"Why, isn't that Unjusa Temple?"

I looked at him with a surprised expression.

"Yes, indeed. They are paintings of the main hall of Unjusa Temple. But look closely at the pictures. In one the fish of the wind bell on the west eaves has gone away somewhere, it's missing; the other is a picture showing the fish hanging there."

Indeed, in one picture the fish below the wind bell was gone, it was not there. That was exactly the spot where I had once been hanging. I looked at him with yet greater surprise.

"I went to Unjusa Temple last autumn to paint. I could not help being surprised on discovering that the fish of the wind bell at the tip of the western eaves of the main hall had gone away somewhere and was missing. I was curious as to why the fish had left, so I asked the fish of the wind bell at the tip of the eastern eaves. At that, he said that his name was Black Bubble-Eyes, and that you had turned into a flying fish and gone flying away. He did not know where you had gone. Then Black Bubble-Eyes, with tears welling in his black eyes, asked me to paint a picture in which you had come back and were once again hanging beneath the bell. He said he wanted to be with you by the picture, at least. And then you might really come back. Many people had visited Unjusa Temple since you left, but not one of them had noticed you were gone. I was the only one who had noticed and asked him about it, so he was making that request . . . I could not refuse Black Bubble-Eyes's request. So these are the paintings I painted last autumn. The fish in that picture is you. Now, what about you going back to your original place, without me having any need to take this picture down to Black Bubble-Eyes? He's surely still waiting for you to come back."

Ah, Black Bubble-Eyes!

I collapsed onto the floor of the studio, calling his name in my heart.

Ah, he was waiting for me so long . . .

The heart of Black Bubble-Eyes waiting for me spread through my heart like ink soaking into rice paper.

I stared up at white, snow-covered Inwangsan Mountain for a while, then rose abruptly.

I must go flying off. I must go flying off to Unjusa Temple immediately. I cannot roam the streets of Seoul any longer. What I have not yet lost is the loving heart of Black Bubble-Eyes. Clearly it was the sound of the Jogyesa wind bell that had made me realize it.

I must go flying off. I must love right now.

I went flying toward the painting that the painter had shown me. Toward the main hall of Unjusa Temple. Towards the place at the tip of the eaves where I had previously been hanging.

The next day at dawn, the monks of Unjusa Temple performed the early morning chanting, yet none of them realized that I had come back and was once again hanging from the tip of the eaves. Only Black Bubble-Eyes had seen that I was back and was smiling brightly.

The sound of Black Bubble-Eyes's bell was clearer and calmer than before. The dawn moonlight that caressed Unjusa Temple was also smiling to see me. A shooting star, too, waved a hand as it vanished in the direction of Jirisan Mountain.

"I'm sorry, Black Bubble-Eyes."

I spoke first.

"Not at all, no need to apologize. I'm so glad you're back. I can't tell you how much I've been waiting for you."

"I know. Forgive me."

"Forgive you? For what?"

I earnestly begged him to forgive me.

"I knew when you got back last night. But as soon as you arrived, you fell into a deep sleep and I guessed you must be utterly exhausted to sleep like that, so I did not want to wake you."

Black Bubble-Eyes's love was, as ever, weighty and deep, like a rock.

"You must have felt so much resentment toward me."

"Not so, Blue Bubble-Eyes. I am grateful to you. You enabled me to know myself. Thanks to you I was able to see myself as I really am. My true self is in your heart, and you have come back to me."

"The same is true for me, too. I have come to know who I am and where I am. I am in your heart, and you waited for me."

"So far I have only loved you outwardly. I am so glad that now I am able to love you inwardly, projected into your heart."

"Thank you so much, Black Bubble-Eyes. If there is any beauty in my life, it is not formed by myself but by your love for me."

I looked straight at Black Bubble-Eyes. In his black gaze a loving heart was visible, flowing like a river. While time had given birth to time, and time had governed that new-born time, we had been separated from each other, unable to meet, but our love for one another had remained unchanged.

"I thought that I would gain a better life if I left here. I thought I could live a more creative life once away from the formal life I was living. But it was not so. I had forgotten one of the most important things. I did not understand that no matter how formal a life one lives, it can be a creative life so long as there is true love in it."

"I thought it was love to let you go away as you wanted. Being with you was love, of course, but I thought it was love to let you go when you wanted to leave. But after you left I have never stopped chiming for a single day. I reckoned that the sound of my bell was the sound of my heart reaching out toward you. By letting you go, I hoped to meet you again."

"You must have been terribly lonely."

"I was lonely, but I still had my waiting. Waiting gave birth to courage, and courage gave birth to patience."

"I failed horribly in loving. Look at my body. I've lost all my scales."

"Blue Bubble-Eyes, no matter what kind of loving it may be, there is no failure in loving. To think that you failed is to think that you did not really love. In every kind of loving there is only success. If I truly loved, that was in itself a success."

Black Bubble-Eyes reached out a hand and gently stroked my scale-less body. His touch was so warm that I wept inwardly.

"Thank you, Black Bubble-Eyes."

"No need to say thank you. As the recumbent Buddha always says: Get rid of me and seek me. Getting rid of your scales was a way of getting rid of yourself. And so you found yourself. Once spring comes, your scales will grow back again, so don't be too sad."

The early morning moon had finally disappeared after listening to us for a while, and now it was the sunshine that was listening to our words.

The wind came blowing. For a while we chimed with warm sounds, caressing one other.

"Today, the sound of the wind bells is exceptionally

warming. Has something happened?"

One of the monks coming out from breakfast looked up at the eaves:

"Aha, you wretch! You're back. Where have you been all this time? Have you learned something about life? Ha ha."

The monk flapped the hem of his robes and burst out laughing.

"I'm sorry, monk."

In my heart I prayed the monk to forgive me.

The sunlight tickled the snow piled up in Unjusa Temple. The ticklish snow gradually melted. The snow was melting along the snowbound path leading up to the recumbent Buddhas. They had come back from their stroll and were lying in their places on the rock slab.

My heart went up to them and greeted them humbly.

"You've had a really hard time . . . but now you're back."

The husband Buddha rose for a moment, patted me on the back, then lay down again.

I wept copious tears. The Buddha's eyebrows were shining white, for the snow covering them had not yet melted.

"So now do you know who you are?"

"Yes, Recumbent Buddha."

"Life as a wind bell is the essence of your life. You are a fish, not a bird. Forgive yourself."

"Yes, Buddha."

"Life is time. It is also a physical time. Live diligently. Living diligently is real life, otherwise it's not life at all. Isn't the wind blowing just for you?"

"Yes, Buddha."

"If you are a flowering tree, you must live as the pale, beautiful roots that bring the flowers into bloom, rather than as the flowers."

"Yes, Buddha. But I want to ask one more thing. What can exist in this world forever?"

"Nothing exists forever. It's really sad. But therefore many things can exist. Only one thing, love, exists forever."

"Then what is the most important thing in our lives?"

Oh, why do I still have so many questions? Does life consist of asking questions?

"In the end it's love. Being without love is like being a bird with no wings. For a wind bell fish like you, it's hanging there with no wind blowing. What causes the most pain in our lives? What makes us suffer the most?

What is the cause of pain and suffering? Think carefully. In the end, isn't it love? Blue Bubble-Eyes, why have you suffered so much? Was it not because of love? In our lives there are things we need and things we want. These two may seem to be the same, but they are different. We go on living even without what we want, but we cannot live without what we need. So, Blue Bubble-Eyes, what is the most necessary thing in life?"

"It is love, Buddha."

"Oh yes, indeed yes, you are right, Blue Bubble-Eyes. It is love. I love you."

The sunshine dies and winter rain falls. Lightning flashes. Thunder echoes through Unjusa Temple as though to scolding me for my folly. The husband Buddha turns on his side and raises a hand to protect his wife's face from the cold winter rain pouring down.

I know that when the rain stops, spring will soon come. Just as love is everlasting in this world, so too is the coming of spring. When spring arrives, Black Bubble-Eyes and I will produce the most beautiful, clear chimes in the world.

Lonely people, come to Unjusa Temple. You who are suffering pain, come to Unjusa Temple. Ah, and above all, you lovers who love one other, come here together.

To hear the chimes Black Bubble-Eyes and I make together . . .

The Sound of the Wind Chime Hanging
from the Eaves of a Poet's Heart

Kim Yong Taik (poet)

The sky is too blue to be true. My eyes looking up at the sky ache, my brow grows sore. I'm quietly gazing at the hill in front of me. It's like a wind chime hanging from an invisible string. If someone strong suddenly raises it, immediately the most beautiful sound that the wind chime had been cherishing rings out and spreads across the blue sky, leading people to peace.

Returning from a visit
to the recumbent Buddhas at Unjusa Temple,
you brought back with you
a wind-chime, hanging

from the eaves of your breast.
If a breeze comes blowing from afar
and you hear the wind-bell chiming,
understand that my heart,
longing to see you,
has come visiting.

This is a poem titled "Hanging Up a Wind Chime" from Jeong Ho-seung's poetry collection *I Am Human Because I Am Lonely*. My favorite line in this poem is the expression "from the eaves of your breast." Jeong Ho-seung is someone who has a wind chime emitting a beautiful sound suspended from his aching breast, like a building's eaves at a street corner where the wind passes. Jeong Ho-seung has always been caressing our sadness, loneliness, and wounded souls with warm hands, with the sound of the wind chime hidden in his heart. When the wind of the world passes over his eaves, his wind chime makes countless sounds.

When an adult reads the tale *Loving*, it serves to send ringing and spreading across the world the sound of the wind chime that Jeong Ho-seung has long cherished and stored up in his breast. What is love? He says it is when people give to their loved ones whatever they have treasured most. Giving and giving, then feeling sorry because there is nothing left to give, that is the heart of love. Indeed so. Anyone always longing to give more to a loved one and at a loss of how to give more will receive something more to give to that loved one if they read this book. As I read this tale, I found myself obliged to stand looking up at the sky for a long time as I fell into the illusion of hearing the sound of a wind chime ringing out in the blue sky for the first time in the world. The tale *Loving* read by adults is the story of the protagonist Blue Bubble-Eyes, who seeks the sound of the wind chime of true love hidden somewhere in our hearts.

Blue Bubble-Eyes started life as a wind chime hanging from the eaves of Unjusa Temple. One day, when she saw a baby swallow falling from the eaves, she was unexpectedly given an opportunity to escape from the wire holding her. Blue Bubble-Eyes, having saved the baby swallow and finding herself turned into a flying fish, goes flying off toward the world, thinking she has gained total freedom.

The first place she heads for is the sea. However, after losing to a hawk the white plover that was accompanying her to the "island that makes the sea beautiful,"

Blue Bubble-Eyes experiences death for the first time in her life. Frightened, she calls to the recumbent Buddhas in Unjusa Temple by starlight. They comfort her and tell her that "death is part of life." The Buddhas appear as starlight whenever Blue Bubble-Eyes is in trouble.

Having lost the white plover, Blue Bubble-Eyes meets a poet. The poet tells her that love happens at first sight, and love is everything in life. Blue Bubble-Eyes now goes to Seoul and meets a gray pigeon, saying, "Seoul is beautiful because you are here." She falls for the wounded pigeon. However, after witnessing the accidental death of Dasom, a child attending kindergarten, Blue Bubble-Eyes, who has faced various trials, recalls Black Bubble-Eyes, the wind-chime fish who was her first love, and experiences a feeling of "a corner of the heart growing bright like day dawning,"

Blue Bubble-Eyes, having left Seoul and traveled around the country, nearly dies many times. She is captured in a restaurant serving steamed carp, then caught on a fishing hook in a reservoir, and also serves to tell fortunes together with a finch. At a stall selling baked carp-cakes she almost dies, then finally understands that she should "Love those whom you must love immediately. Don't put it off until tomorrow."

Coming back to Seoul, Blue Bubble-Eyes falls deeply in love with the gray pigeon she had first met there. Then one day, a silver dove appears and falls in love with the gray pigeon. Blue Bubble-Eyes calls out to the recumbent Buddhas in Unjusa Temple and they comfort her by saying, "There is no beauty in this world without wounds." Blue Bubble-Eyes accidentally meets an artist who has painted Unjusa Temple and learns that Black Bubble-Eyes still loves her. So she returns to Unjusa Temple and recognizes the true love of Black Bubble-Eyes.

The pilgrimage of Blue Bubble-Eyes in search of love is a rite of passage that everything in the world must pass through. There is no love without the pain of parting. Every beautiful love in this world is a wounded love. Where in this world is there a green pine tree without a wound? Only those who have passed through "festivals of pain," dark plains of despair and longing, in order to attain true love can smile brightly at the world.

Loving is therefore a message of love and peace. Jeong Ho-seung shows us through Blue Bubble-Eyes that the place we should finally come back to is the eaves of love. Therefore, *Loving* is the sound of the wind chime of love that rings and spreads among us who are living in this "poor era" which seems to lack nothing.

The sound of the wind chime he sends echoing will make our hearts and ears clean. The sound of his wind chime is not an alarm for the world, but the sound of a wind chime looking for love, so we will be astonished to discover hidden in our hearts the sound of a wind chime soft like the sound of a blade of grass and send it ringing and spreading through the heavens like the white snowflakes of winter. So those who have been wounded by love and weep will find bright love like snow falling on top of the painful wounds, while those anxious about love will gain joyful love as if it comes hastening right now, and those without love will be soaked with love until their eyes open to love.

Those who are in love, open the door now for it has come. There, the sound of the wind chime on the eaves of the poet's breast, in the snow falling without any wind—it is standing like a snowman under the falling white snow, will love and smile, all white. Then approach and brush away the snow on his shoulders, his head. And as you set off in search of the sound of a wind chime, you will hear the whispering sound of the poet Jeong Ho-seung, who loves the world supremely, saying: Love right now, Love is the most beautiful reality. And finally, he will sing to us like snowflakes falling without wind, telling us to love like this.

Now, no matter whom you love,
love someone who knows when autumn leaves fall.
Now, no matter whom you love,
love someone who knows why autumn leaves fall to
    lowly places.
Now, no matter whom you love,
love someone who can fall like one autumn leaf.
On days when October's red moon has set
and you long for a warm glow outside your window,
no matter whom you love,
love someone who can fall and rot like one autumn
    leaf,
love someone who can rot as one autumn leaf
and wait for spring to come again.

The shadow of the hill falls across the playground and the sun sets. Birds have gone flying off. I must go home now. There is a wind chime in my heart too, and I must make the wind chime ring out for one whom I love. Ah, what better thing can there be than having someone to love in this world? It is peace, rest, the last and the first thing in this world.